Bright Skies and Dark Horses

BRIGHT SKIES AND DARK HORSES

WESTERN STORIES

JOHN D. NESBITT

FIVE STAR

A part of Gale, a Cengage Company

GALE
A Cengage Company

LIBRARY OF CONGRESS CATALOGING-IN-PUBLICATION DATA

Names: Nesbitt, John D., author.
Title: Bright skies and dark horses / John D Nesbitt.
Description: First edition. | Waterville, Maine: Five Star, 2023. | Identifiers: LCCN 2022019475 | ISBN 9781432899127 (hardcover)
Subjects: LCGFT: Western fiction. | Short stories.
Classification: LCC PS3564.E76 B75 2023 | DDC 813/.54—dc23/eng/20220425
LC record available at https://lccn.loc.gov/2022019475

First Edition. First Printing: February 2023
Find us on Facebook—https://www.facebook.com/FiveStarCengage
Visit our website—http://www.gale.cengage.com/fivestar
Contact Five Star Publishing at FiveStar@cengage.com

Printed in Mexico
Print Number: 1   Print Year: 2023

For my grey horse Pearl

ACKNOWLEDGMENTS

"Incident at Blue Nose Creek" appeared in *Saddlebag Dispatches,* Summer 2021, where it took second place in the Flash Fiction contest.

"In the Breaks" appeared in *The Spoilt Quilt and Other Frontier Stories* (Waterville, ME: Five Star Publishing, 2019).

"Night Horse" appeared in *Six-Gun Justice* anthology, ed. Richard Prosch, 2021.

"Buckskin Ruby" appeared in *Rope and Wire* (online magazine), April 2021.

CONTENTS

CONTENTS

★ ★ ★ ★ ★

Incident at
Blue Nose Creek

★ ★ ★ ★ ★

Rhodes found the ranch at Blue Nose Creek, where the cotton-wood trees were turning yellow and the grass had gone pale and dry. At a bend in the stream, three white canvas tents shimmered beneath a blue sky. Up the slope a hundred yards, the ranch yard sat silent as smoke threaded from a stovepipe in the bunkhouse roof. Rhodes nudged his horse that way.

The bunkhouse door opened, and a man in a drab hat and work clothes stepped outside. "What do you want?"

Rhodes dismounted. "I'd like to talk to the person in charge."

"That's me. I'm the foreman."

"Pleased to meet you. My name's Bob Rhodes. I was wondering if I could put up for a day or two. My horse could use a rest. I'd be glad to work for my keep."

The foreman's eyes traveled over Rhodes and his horse. "I suppose so. We've got other company that takes supper with us. Group of surveyors. They're camped down there."

"I saw the tents."

"The cook could use the help. I'll tell him. You can put your horse in the corral."

After supper, with the dishes cleaned and put away, Rhodes looked for a seat. Two ranch hands were playing cribbage at the middle of the long table. At the end near the sheet iron stove, three of the surveyors and their camp tender were playing a game of pinochle. The fourth surveyor, whose name Rhodes had caught as Chambers, sat apart facing the stove.

The man was above average height and sat straight in his chair. He had brown hair, beginning to grey at the temples, and a trimmed mustache. He wore wire-rimmed spectacles as he read a newspaper and smoked a straight stem pipe. His corduroy trousers were tucked into his long brown boots, and his dust colored canvas field coat was closed above the waist with rounded leather buttons.

Rhodes said, "You fellas must get to see a lot of good country."

One of the pinochle players said, "Some of it."

"Where-all have you been?"

"Various places in Colorado before we came here."

Chambers gave a sideways glance. "Why do you care?"

"Oh, I travel around, work here and there. I like to learn about the country." When no one spoke, Rhodes turned to the pinochle player and said, "How long have you fellas been workin' together?"

"A while."

"I'm sorry. I shouldn't pester you. I know you're more interested in the queen of spades and the jack of diamonds right now."

No one answered. Chambers set down his paper, produced a steel-handled penknife, and opened it. He scraped the bowl of his pipe with the short blade.

Rhodes said, "I'm on my way to Montana. I've got a job waiting for me that should carry me through the winter."

The camp tender said, "Gets cold up there."

Rhodes smiled. "That's the good of it. I'll be cuttin' wood." He cast a casual glance at Chambers as the surveyor kept his blue grey eyes on the blade. The man had strong-looking hands. Rhodes gave a quick review of the places where saloon girls had turned up dead—Colorado Springs, Longmont, Fort Morgan.

The name and the description matched, and the surveyor with the trimmed mustache and firm facial muscles did nothing to make Rhodes think otherwise.

Rhodes stood outside the faint glow of light that came through the wall of the tent. He heard the voices of the surveyors and their tender, but because of the placement of the lantern, he could not see their shadows. They were making small talk, and he gathered that they were passing around a bottle. Rhodes listened for Chambers, expecting to hear the man make a comment about the chap who asked too many questions in the bunkhouse, but he could not pick out the man's voice.

Rhodes shifted his attention to his surroundings. A faint gurgle came from the creek. He thought he heard the sound of a night bird leaving a branch, but as he looked up and around in the light of the half moon, he saw nothing. He felt for his pistol in the cross-draw holster beneath his jacket, and he moved his left foot to be sure of the knife he carried in his boot.

He frowned. He did not know if he had heard the flap of a wing or some other—

A jolt of fear ran through him to his heels as a cord tightened on his throat and pulled him back. His hat tumbled away. He squirmed and dropped, breaking the man's hold, but Chambers closed in on him, got his arms around him, and slammed him to the ground. He landed on his back. He smelled a trace of whiskey as Chambers sat on his chest, knees athwart, and settled the strong hands on his throat.

This is the way he does it.

Rhodes thrashed, felt for his pistol, and could not find it. Desperate, as light flashed behind his eyelids, he bucked and heaved. Chambers tipped to one side, and Rhodes twisted his shoulder enough to reach the knife in its scabbard in his boot.

He brought the knife up flat along his leg, between them,

until he bucked again and was able to move the blade upward. He held the handle tight, and as Chambers lunged to force his weight down, Rhodes drove the blade home.

The hands relaxed on his throat as a long, guttering breath spent itself and Chambers slumped.

Rhodes's hand was wet and sticky, dark in the moonlight, as he pushed the dying man away. He rolled over onto his knees and lifted his head. The other men had come out of the tent and stood near in the moonlight.

"What's going on?"

"What happened here?"

"Why did you do that?"

Rhodes stood up. "I'm an investigator. I'll tell you the story as soon as I can catch my breath."

★ ★ ★ ★ ★

VISITORS IN CANTERA

★ ★ ★ ★ ★

I was brushing my donkey under a late spring sky, with warm weather making a pretense after a few days of cold rains, when I thought I heard a sound. I stopped to listen but heard nothing more. A dry breeze carried through the backyard, where sunlight slanted down but did not do away with the chill. The town of Cantera could have a desolate quality at any season, as a person might hear the rapping of a hammer from across town. But silence returned, and I enjoyed the company of Pedro, who pulled on the lead rope as he kept his head low to crop grass. Donkeys do not all shed in the springtime as horses do, so I was currying hard against his brownish-black wool and not thinking about much when a loud, shrill woman's voice sounded.

"*Yoo-hoo! Yoo-hoo!* Anyone home?"

A man's voice followed. "Anyone home?"

Nothing seemed familiar, neither their voices nor their manner of calling. Thinking they might be travelers, I did not lose time. With the steel currycomb in hand, I led my donkey out front to meet my visitors.

A man and a woman stood a few steps away from the front door. At first glance, I could not have said that they looked like a couple except that they had a similar dowdy appearance of having been in the same clothes for a few days straight. The man was of average height, wearing a short-brimmed brown hat and a suit of a matching color. He had clear eyes, a trimmed mustache, and a couple of days' stubble. He made a half-smile and nodded.

The woman wore a loose-fitting dress and an open sweater, plus a wide-brimmed hat that kept her pale face in shade. I could see that she had puffy eyelids and a wide mouth, along with sagging folds of flesh that fell from her chin to her throat.

"We knocked and knocked," she said, in a tone of complaint.

"I'm sorry I didn't hear you. I was out back, and sometimes the wind comes in from the alley and carries the sound the other way." I took in both of them. "How can I help you?"

The woman spoke. "Is this your mule?"

"He's a donkey. His name is Pedro." I waited for them to state their business, and after a few seconds I said, "Are you interested in a room?"

"Are you Owen Gregor?" she asked.

"Yes, I am. And this is my lodging house. Not to make any assumptions, but I thought you might be travelers."

I had the impression that the man, although he was more alert than the woman, was waiting for her to do the talking. After a few more seconds, her mouth moved. She made a nervous sound, like a light laugh, and then spoke.

"I don't know how to tell you this, but I'm your cousin."

I took a new look at her, to see if I could find something familiar, but nothing registered.

"My mother was Mary Frances Wendling. She was a sister to your mother, who was Margaret. Am I right?"

"Yes, that was my mother's name."

"Then we're cousins. My name is Ida."

My eyes roved over her again. I did not want to stare at her, but I was trying to find something that would fit into place. "So, did you come from Davenport?"

"No. I haven't lived in Iowa for a long time. For that matter, we've come from California. This is my husband, Floyd."

The man and I turned toward each other, stepped forward, and shook hands.

"Floyd Corliss."

"Pleased to meet you. I'm Owen Gregor, as you already know. And this is my lodging house. I'm used to travelers, and I'd be happy to have you stay over." His face tensed, and I said, "No charge, of course." As soon as I said it, I wondered if I had fallen in too soon. I turned to Ida and said, "I'm sorry if I didn't know you, but I don't recall my mother having mentioned you. I know she had a sister named Mary Frances, though." A vague memory rose in my mind, of things not discussed.

"I never had much family. Just my mother and me. And it was never easy."

"I'm sorry to hear that." I smiled. "I don't know what kind of a relative I'll turn out to be, but I leave that to you." For the first time, I wondered how they saw me, a man of middle height and middle age in a dust-colored, battered hat, a shirt to match, and denim trousers, holding a donkey in a world where cattle-men were kings and rode fine horses.

"You don't have any brothers or sisters, do you?" she said.

"No, I don't."

"Then you're the only cousin I've got."

I did not have an answer. I glanced around and said, "Do you have luggage somewhere? Do we need to fetch it?"

Ida blurted, "Your mule could carry it. Ha-ha-ha-ha-ha-ha-ha-ha."

Floyd drew his brows together. "It's a donkey, dear."

"Of course it is."

He turned to me. "We don't have that much. We can carry it."

I gave a little shrug. "I could fit him out, but it would take a

21

while for such a little task. I'll be glad to help you carry your bags."

"That's very kind of you," he said.

We gathered in the sitting room after Ida and Floyd had their luggage settled in their room. I noticed that Floyd, with his hat off, had a full head of brown hair, while his mustache was going to grey. Ida had mouse-colored hair and at least as many folds and wrinkles as I had seen in the shadow of her hat. I guessed his age at about fifty and hers at four or five years less, but he appeared to be in much better condition. Neither of them seemed to be an invalid, so I offered them a drink.

"I have about half a bottle of wine on hand," I said, "and the better half of a bottle of whiskey."

Ida spoke right up. "I'll have the wine. I can't drink whiskey. It's too hard. But I can drink wine."

Floyd smiled. "The whiskey sounds all right to me."

I served their drinks, poured myself a glass to match Floyd's, and took a seat with them in the front room. I had drawn back the curtains, so the sunlight streamed in and gave us a warm, cheery atmosphere.

Floyd took a sip of his whiskey. He had a relaxed air about him. He smiled again and said, "This is a nice, quiet little business you have."

"Quiet is right. In my parents' time, there was quite a bit more activity in this town."

"It seems to have a deserted feeling to it."

"Yes, it does. You can see the old businesses shut up. There are still ranches in the surrounding area, and the town has business from that, but at one time, there were a couple of quarries that were booming and bustling. That's how the town got its name. Cantera means quarry."

"I didn't know that."

"Yes, but the demand for stone went down, and one of the quarry owners had a great sadness when his son drowned in a water trough, and things dwindled away."

"That's too bad. Not much opportunity here. Doesn't look as if things change very much."

"They don't. We had some excitement—you might say turmoil—a little over a year ago. A man named Dunbar came to town, and we learned that he was investigating the death of the quarry owner's son from many years before."

"Oh."

"It turned out that the town marshal had been responsible for the boy's death, but another man went to prison for it. When the truth came out, the marshal put up a fight and then turned fugitive. He had bought the other abandoned quarry, and he went out that way. Dunbar followed him, and to make a short story of it, the marshal fell into a deep pit with slick sides and a deadly pool at the bottom."

Floyd raised his eyebrows. "That would be an interesting place to see."

Ida tittered her glass, which was almost empty. "Not with me along. Ha-ha-ha-ha-ha."

I said, "The bank has taken it over. It used a quantity of the stone to make some repairs, and then the banker had a dynamiter come and fill in the pit with rubble. Ted, the barber, was taking sightseers out there, making money off of visitors."

Floyd pursed his lips. "It's just as well. To close it down, that is."

"It was a dangerous place, with snakes as well."

Ida spoke up. "The banker didn't like him making money."

I answered. "There could have been some of that. But Ted's not a bad sort. We went past his place when we brought your luggage."

"I saw it," said Floyd.

We sat in the front room for a while, with no one in a hurry, as we chatted about the weather and about the various ways people made a living in this area. The sunlight moved. Floyd had a second glass of whiskey. Ida finished off the wine. When the shadows were beginning to lengthen outside, I said that I needed to step out and buy some provisions for supper.

"We're doing fine here," said Floyd. "Resting up after our travel."

"Very good. Is there anything else I should get?" I turned to Ida, and her mouth opened, but she did not speak. I said, "I don't know if I can find any more wine. I usually have to order it. Is there anything else you might like to drink?"

"Gin," she said. "I can drink gin."

Ida and Floyd sat in the kitchen as I built a fire in the cookstove and worked on the meal. After a while I had pork chops sizzling in one skillet and potatoes frying in another. Floyd was keeping the same pace with his whiskey as he had on his first two glasses, and Ida was serving the gin herself.

She took up her earlier theme about how sad and lonely it was to grow up and not have a family. I noticed that she and Floyd did not mention how long they had been together or whether either of them had ever had children. I did not ask any personal questions. As a general rule, I prefer not to be inquisitive, and in this case, I did not care to know.

The sentiment seemed to be mounting in her, however. She had become teary-eyed and blubbering, and I had been able to keep a shoulder to her, until she rose from her chair and put her arms around me. "You don't know what it's like," she said. "You always had someone. I never had anyone."

"That's all right." I tried to edge away, but she held onto me. She had been speaking into my ear, and now she was just sobbing.

Floyd had risen from his chair as well and stood near. He was paying close attention, as if he wanted to hear anything she said.

She did not divulge anything, though. Between sobs, she said, "You're the only family I have. I never knew you, but I always knew you were out there. You're like my brother."

I felt myself resisting, but I kept myself from pushing her away. I did not know what she wanted, but I hoped it was not to have them both stay on as long-term guests.

Floyd took her by the arm and said, "Let's sit down, dear. Let him cook the meal. We have plenty of time to talk."

"I know. I know."

He seemed intent on keeping her under control, lest she say something inconvenient, but I did not see anything sinister. I did notice, however, that his hair was grey at the roots. I had not stood that close to him before.

I had a fire going in the stove again the next morning when Floyd made his appearance. He had shaved—with cold water, I assumed—and had put on a clean shirt. He was clear-eyed and did not seem the worse from the night before.

"Ida needs more sleep than I do," he said. "This climate is supposed to be good for people in her condition, but it doesn't seem that helpful."

"We've had damp weather. I expect it to warm up and dry out."

He took a seat at the table, calm as before. He sat at a right angle to me as I sliced bacon for the skillet. "Have you always lived by yourself?" he asked.

"Well, yes. Since my parents passed on. But I do have a prospect. A lady friend of mine, name of Emilia, has agreed to a plan of joining our houses."

"Marriage?"

"Um, yes. I don't go around talking about it a great deal, but that's the idea. But we also intend to join things in a literal way. She has a little house that she won't need, and we plan to make an addition here with the lumber."

"You sure won't be cramped for room."

"I don't think so, though she has a brother she takes care of."

"Cripple?"

"No, not that. He is full-grown and gets around, but I would say he does not have full mental capacities. He needs someone to take care of him, and Emilia is very good in all those ways."

"I see."

I laid the strips of bacon in the skillet and began to mix the pancake batter. I had the sense, as I had the night before, that my visitors were sounding out the possibility of staying for a while, and I didn't mind being able to discourage them and to tell the truth at the same time.

The coffee boiled, and I set it to one side to let the grounds settle. I spooned some bacon grease into the second skillet and poured in enough batter for one large hotcake.

"I've got butter and chokecherry syrup," I said.

"That's good. We had chokecherry syrup in Colorado."

I brought the butter and syrup from the pantry and served him the first brown hotcake with three strips of bacon.

"This is first-rate," he said.

"I've got plenty of batter. Do you think you'll want a second one?"

He studied his plate and nodded. "I believe I can eat two."

I cooked the second hotcake, poured coffee, and cooked a short stack of two for myself. As I settled into my seat to have my meal, I asked him what kind of work he did. I thought I was making light conversation and not being as personal as he had been with me.

He went on to tell a roundabout story about working for an

26

insurance firm in Sacramento, where he was pushed out to make room for a son-in-law, which sent him to working as a sales clerk, mainly in clothing, though he would have liked to have gotten into photography, but the equipment was too expensive. So he and the wife, as he now called her, decided they would like to travel, which they had always wanted to do, and he was on the lookout for a good position.

I asked him what kind of business he would like to get into, and he said he thought he would do well as a hotel manager. He had a good head for business, and he wouldn't have to worry about rent. But he knew those jobs were hard to find, and he thought he might do well at barbering while he looked for a better position. He realized they would have to find a larger town for that.

"I think so," I said. "The only business that resembles a hotel in this town is the boarding house, and it has limited possibilities. As for barbering, Ted has a firm hold on that business."

"So it seems."

I finished my meal and poured more coffee for the two of us. As I was sitting down, Ida flowed into the kitchen in a cloud of what I thought was some kind of mouthwash.

"Good morning," she said, in what seemed to be an effort to sound cheerful.

I stood up. "How are you?"

She sighed. "As well as can be expected. My rheumatism is killing me. It doesn't let me sleep for half the night."

"Maybe you'll feel better if you have something to eat. What do you think about breakfast?"

"I'd like some eggs if you have them."

I realized I had not asked my question well enough, but I did have some eggs on hand, so I cooked a pair for her and served them on a plate along with some bacon I had fried earlier. As I set the food in front of her, I saw that I had not offered her any coffee, as I had been a bit perturbed at having to let the batter go to waste.

"Would you like some coffee?" I asked.

"Sure."

I poured her a cup. "Would you like anything with it?"

"Cream and sugar."

I perforated a can of milk with an ice pick and set the can and the sugar bowl next to her cup.

She had been dawdling with her bacon and eggs. She set down her fork, picked up a spoon, added sugar to her coffee, and poured in a dose of canned milk. She blew across the surface, although the coffee was not that hot now, and drank about a quarter of the contents.

"I could take some of that whiskey," she said. "This is the only way I can drink it. But it helps me with the pain."

As I took the whiskey bottle from the cupboard, I saw that the gin bottle was not where I had left it. I told myself not to worry, that once it was gone, it was gone.

I let her pour her own medicine, but I stood by. I turned to swish at a fly so that I would not watch her take a drink. I felt an annoyance rising in me, and I made myself be civil. I took a seat at the table again.

"Have you been enjoying your travels?" I asked.

She was poking at her food and eating very little of it. "This climate and elevation are supposed to be good for my rheumatism, but I'm in pain all the time. I wish I could work, but every time I find a job, the rheumatism gets me down."

The idea of her working struck my curiosity. "What kind of work do you do?"

"I've done office work. Secretary and clerk. That was how I met Floyd, in an insurance office. I knew as much about the business as anyone who worked there, but they would never let me be an agent or do sales."

Floyd was watching her close, and he found an opening when she reached for her coffee. "Well, Owen, have you lived here all your life?"

I was tempted to say, "Not yet," but that had been Dunbar's joke, and I answered the question straight. "I grew up here with my parents, went out into the world, got into some trouble, and made my way back. By then the town had declined, as I mentioned yesterday."

Ida said, "But you still have a business here. You make a living, don't you?"

I began to answer, but she interrupted.

"Don't mind me. I'm always asking the wrong questions. Ha-ha-ha-ha-ha-ha-ha-ha-ha."

Her laugh was like a mechanical toy that she let go and then stopped. I took a deep breath. Seeing her empty cup, I asked if she would like some more coffee.

"I'd love some."

"Same as before?" I got up to pour the coffee.

"Yes, please. It's made me feel better."

I left room in the cup for her to pour the whiskey, and I took my seat again.

She took a drink, gave out a long "ahhh," and said, "At least I didn't ask you what you got in trouble for." In a quick change to a self-deprecating tone, she said, "I'm sorry."

"It's no secret. Anyone in town, or at least anyone who has lived here a while, could tell you. I was young and didn't have good judgment. I held the horses for a couple of fellows who thought they knew how to rob a train. They told me that if anything happened, they'd keep me out of it, but of course they didn't."

Floyd said, "Well, you came back and did well for yourself."

He sounded like one genteel felon speaking to another. I said, "I've gotten by. But I paid for my mistake, ten years, and I make an honest living, such as it is."

"Nothing wrong with that," said Ida. "There's a lot of rich bitches can't say that."

"She means men," Floyd put in. "That's just her way of speaking."

"I understand."

Ida continued. "People who have all the money keep it. Most of it isn't theirs to begin with."

I frowned. I imagined she had some theory or rationale behind the statement, but I did not understand it.

Floyd moved in to steer the topic again. He told a story about their visit to Deadwood. They saw a man who had won a great deal of money being protected by armed guards who worked there. "They let people watch him collect the money, but they kept them at a distance."

I thought I was beginning to understand my visitors after all, and I was glad that I didn't have much for them to covet. I asked if they would like to sit in the backyard in the sunshine while I cleaned up the kitchen.

Ida said, "I'm all right here. I love to watch other people work. Ha-ha-ha-ha-ha."

I understood that, too. She had a third slug of whiskey while I washed the dishes and put things away. Floyd sat with his usual repose.

When I had everything in order, the three of us went into the backyard. I let Pedro out of his pen and held him on a lead rope as he cropped the new grass.

Ida and Floyd sat in their wooden armchairs. She was relaxed and dull, and she slurred her words as she muttered how lovable the donkey was. Floyd was clear and alert. He took out a cigarette and lit it, the only one I had seen him smoke during their visit so far.

Ida began to blubber again about never having a family and

about how hard she had always had it, even now. I was afraid she was going to get up and try to hug me again, but she seemed sunk into her chair. Her voice rose as she said, "But we can't just stay here with you. I know you have things to do, I heard you tell Floyd, and we don't want to wear out our welcome."

"Not at all," said Floyd, tapping his ash. "We need to be on our way in a day or two."

I found the empty gin bottle in their room. I was glad they were gone, but I think I had to convince myself, because I took Pedro out front to brush him, as if I had to keep an eye out to make sure they weren't coming back.

Much better, Emilia appeared, dark-haired in a dark dress, walking from the center of town to the edge where my lodging house sat across from the empty Emporium.

"Are your visitors gone?" she asked.

"Yes, they are."

"Were you happy to see someone from your family?"

"I hadn't thought of it in that way. I have to admit I was glad to see them leave. She rather wore me out."

"That's too bad. But even if you got tired of her, she is still your family, and you have so little."

"That's true. But I can't say that I had very much feeling in that way. She may have, but I couldn't be sure how much. I thought they were looking for an opportunity, some place where they could move in and get along without having to do much. And, I thought, to keep from being found."

Her eyes opened. "Really?"

"Yes. He reminded me of someone I met once. A forger. The fellow stole a great deal of money and then skipped out on his accomplice. So he had more than one party looking for him."

"Oh, your poor cousin."

"I don't know how innocent she is, though I believe he's the

31

worse of the two. I think she has something on him, and he can't get rid of her. He might like to."

"You don't think he would do something to her?"

I laughed. "I don't know. But he seemed interested in the pit that the marshal fell into. It may have been a fancy of his, but she made a joke about it as well."

"You will have to be careful if they come back. Do you think you should find out more about them?"

"I don't think they'll be back. There's no opportunity here. As for finding out more about them, there are ways I could do it. But I don't want to know more. I would have to take the initiative, and then I would wish I hadn't gone that far. Some people, like Mr. Dunbar, can look for the truth and go through great trouble to find it, but they have a higher reason to begin with, I believe."

"Oh, yes. Mr. Dunbar. He was very good. Of course, you are, too."

I smiled and took her hand. "I am nothing by myself. But I have a good woman and a good donkey. What more could I want?"

★ ★ ★ ★ ★

IN THE BREAKS

★ ★ ★ ★ ★

On the first morning in camp, Grandpa had me hold the halter ropes while he saddled the horses. When he pulled the cinch on the first horse, a sorrel named Baldy with a wide, white blaze, the animal reared up and pawed the air, pulling the rope through my hand.

"That cinch is cold," said Grandpa. "The sweat from yesterday froze before it could dry out. He'll be all right, though. We'll let him settle down."

Grandpa went on to saddle the second horse, a larger sorrel with a small patch on the nose, named Snip. The horse did not react to either the front cinch or the rear cinch being tightened.

I continued to hold the horses as Grandpa brought the rifles and scabbards out of the tent and strapped one scabbard onto the saddle of each horse. I watched the whole time, trying to remember all the details. I didn't mind being treated like the sixteen-year-old girl that I was, standing back and letting the grown-up man do the work that took skill, but it was understood that I was learning in order to do these things myself.

Grandpa told me to mount up first, but Baldy kept running out from under me each time I put my foot in the stirrup. I brought him back to the starting point each time and tried again.

"Look here, Katie," said Grandpa. "Lay your reins on the far side of the saddle horn, and pull your left rein so that his head is a quarter-turn in. He won't run on you because he can't follow his head. Now keep hold of both reins as you grab the saddle horn and pull yourself up. Don't grab the back of the saddle. Both hands on the pommel."

I did as I was told, and the next thing I knew, I was sitting in the saddle, and Baldy was standing still.

Grandpa led his horse out a few steps, halted, and got set. He pulled himself up, swung his leg over, and settled in.

The heavyset sorrel began bucking, first in a gentle rocking-horse motion, but when he did not unseat the man on his back, he started bucking higher on both ends. Grandpa hung on as long as he could, but the horse pitched him forward off the right side. Grandpa landed hard on his feet as Snip ran away, bucking and kicking.

"Are you all right?" I asked.

"I think I broke something. I landed crooked on my right foot."

My stomach tightened. "Can you walk?"

"I can move. But I think I broke my ankle." He walked in a circle, half-bent and hobbling, as if he was testing his foot.

"Then I had better go fetch that horse. Do you think I can walk up to him?"

"I think so. He's just standing there. I think he's got it all bucked out of him for the time being. That's just the way it is with some horses on a cold morning."

I slid off of Baldy and handed the reins to Grandpa. With uncertain steps, I walked toward the runaway Snip.

Grandpa was right. The husky sorrel was breathing hard, but he did not have any renegade in him as I laid hold of the rope and led him back to camp.

"What does this do to our hunting?" I asked.

"We still hunt. We don't quit now." He cast a glance at Snip. "I think I can pull myself up into the saddle, and I can ride with you to show you where I had it in mind for us to go. But I don't think I can hunt on foot—least of all in any place that's rough going with downed timber."

I let the realization settle in. "So I'll have to hunt alone? Shoot a deer all by myself?"

"Like I've told you, it's like hunting a rabbit, only bigger."

I felt as if a heavy weight of responsibility was being settled on me all at once. I had left the orphanage in Pennsylvania and had come to live with Grandpa on the ranch just a little more than six months earlier, and I had learned a great many things— how to work around cattle, how to saddle a horse, how to shoot a rifle, and how to clean a rabbit. Now it looked as if I was going to have to take a big step by myself.

Grandpa put all his weight on his left leg, gave a couple of hops, and steadied himself with his right foot. He said, "Don't worry, Katie. We won't starve to death if we don't get a deer, but it'll be nice if we do."

"I know."

"So we'd better get to work, or the morning'll slip away from us. At least Snip here didn't spill the rifle out of the scabbard."

Grandpa was pulling on the front end of the horse to settle him into position when the footfalls of another horse made us turn.

My spirits sank when I recognized Jeff Hayden riding a dull, dark, blocky horse. Jeff had a knack for showing up wherever I was, whether it was on the range, around the ranch yard, or in town. I did not think that his riding up to our camp was a pure coincidence.

He called out in the grey light of morning. "How-de-do, Mr. Cooper. Miss Moran."

Most things about Jeff Hayden galled me, including his constant show of politeness.

"Mornin'," said Grandpa.

I nodded, and Jeff gave me a closed-mouth smile.

"Need any help?" he asked.

Grandpa said, "I don't think so. This boy threw me off, but I need to get back on him, by myself, so he knows I'm still the boss."

"Goin' deer huntin' in the breaks, huh?"

"That's our plan."

"You should do all right. These here blacktail aren't that hard to hunt. Back home, all we've got is whitetail. They'll make you work for it."

I had heard enough of him from before, about coon hunting in Kentucky, and I hoped deep down that I would not have to have anything to do with him in the deer hunt.

"Looks like you're favorin' your foot," he said. "You sure you don't need some help?" Jeff stopped his horse, swung down from the saddle, and strode our way.

As he drew closer, I noted his red hair, blue eyes, pale face, and upturned nose. He did not complicate things by being handsome. I found myself drawing my arms in tight against my sides.

Grandpa did not look straight at him. "We'll be all right on our own. Thanks all the same."

Jeff stopped. "Sure. Just thought I'd offer. I've got the day off, and I thought I might do some huntin' myself. But I can get a deer any time, so if you change your mind, just let me know."

He turned and walked away, leading the dull-colored horse. Ten yards out, he stopped, grabbed the saddle horn with both hands, and swung up into the saddle, stabbing his foot in the stirrup after he left the ground, and swooping with his right leg as he brought it around snug. With a light air he straightened up, tipped his head back, and rode away.

Grandpa went back to pushing his horse into place. I knew Grandpa was stubborn and independent, so I let him strain and pull himself up into the saddle. Snip did not give him any trouble. As Grandpa adjusted his reins, he said, "Go ahead and git mounted."

I had a nervous fluttering in my stomach, but I remembered to hold the left rein snug, and I made it up into the saddle without any incident.

Grandpa let out a long breath. "Well, we got that much done. Let's go see if we can find a deer."

We rode up the slope from our camp, which we had set on a level, grassy area at the edge of the timber on the south side of the Osteen Breaks. The pine and cedar trees grew in some rough, steep places on both sides of the breaks, and trees gave good cover for deer as well as for coyotes, bobcats, porcupines, and an occasional mountain lion. I took Grandpa's word for the mountain lions, but I had seen all the other animals myself. Now I was keeping an eye out for deer.

We followed a trail that I would have thought, when I first came out from the East, was a game trail, but from hoofprints and cow pies I learned that cattle could walk on very narrow and steep paths. This trail angled up the hillside, cut back, and came out on top where it passed between two large rocks. We stopped there.

The breaks consisted of a long pine ridge with countless side canyons and crevices. Up on top, at this place where the trail crossed over, the land spread out, not quite level but not a razorback. This was the spot where Grandpa had decided we would start our hunt.

He took a seat on a large fallen log and held the horses while I made my way into the timber. As Grandpa had explained, the winds blew stronger across the top of the breaks, so I found a great deal of deadfall to crawl over and sometimes under. As the sun began to climb in the morning sky, it sent shafts of light into the standing trees. The hanging pine needles glistened a shiny green, as did the long grass in some of the small, open areas I came to.

From time to time I stopped to let the silence gather as the woods filled in around me. I heard a crow cawing as it flew overhead, and I heard squirrels chattering. I rehearsed what I would do if I saw a deer. I would move to a nearby tree, get a steady rest, and take aim. If the deer had antlers, I would shoot. If it did not, I would decide.

I hunted for more than an hour, moving farther and farther from the place where Grandpa had stayed with the horses. I was not cold at all, though the day had started out frosty. I felt loose and relaxed in my red-and-black-checked hunting jacket. It held in the warmth but did not make me perspire. I liked it for its soft flannel lining, its big pockets, and the pouch in back. It made very little noise when a twig or branch brushed against it.

I stopped near a thick pine tree so that I would not be out in the open. I was hungry already, and I told myself to wait. I reviewed what I had in the pockets of my jacket—two biscuits, a small cloth sack of dried apples, a jackknife with a sharp blade, a folding case of rifle shells, a whistle, matches, a supply of folded newspaper, and a couple of yards of thick string. The whistle was to help someone find me if I got lost. The matches would help me start a fire if I got stranded at night. The newspaper had more than one use. The string would serve to lace up the deer's belly after I took out the innards. That way, I could keep the heart and liver inside and the dirt and leaves and pine needles out. Grandpa had drilled this detail into my head, but it still existed on the hypothetical level for me. The biscuits and dried apples were as real as could be, but I could not let myself eat them when the sun had just climbed to eight o'clock.

Anyway, I guessed it was eight. Grandpa made me leave my dollar watch in the tent. He said a deer could hear it tick, and I should be able to estimate the time anyway. He also told me stories about how easy it was to lose track of time as well as direction when a person was tracking an animal he had shot.

I had plenty of things to think about as I walked and paused, walked and paused, along the ridge of the Osteen Breaks. My thoughts also went back to Grandpa, who I imagined was still waiting with the horses. A year earlier, I would never have thought I would be out here under the wide Wyoming skies, wearing a red-and-black hunting jacket, and carrying a Winchester rifle that went snickety-snick like magic. I had been just one more orphan girl, looked over as a potential chore girl, farm worker, or housekeeper until one day I was told that my grandfather Cooper had traced my whereabouts and was coming to see me.

I could not remember ever being called a pretty girl, or having a pretty dress. The nicest thing I remembered hearing was "She'll be a late bloomer." I felt I was very common, maybe even homely, for people looked me over and then looked over me to the next one. So I must have been a good prospect to go out and be an old man's helper on a homestead of sagebrush, dry grass, and dust.

Still, it was home now, and I could not remember ever having had a home. I was getting used to this way of life, so when Grandpa gave me the old hunting jacket and said, "It's yours now," it all seemed natural.

A tramping sound brought me back to the moment where I was, standing in the pine trees with sunlight slanting in. I heard a few steps, then silence. I could not place where the sound came from. I heard the tramping again, to my right. With the sun at my forehead, I frowned and peered. I saw a patch of color that did not belong to the tree trunks, pine needles, and deadfall—a shadowy dull brown with a tinge of blue. One shape stood in front of another, which in turn stood in front of another. A small file of deer was moving through the timber and had stopped.

I held as still as I could. I needed to wait until the animals gave me a better view, but I needed to be ready if I saw something I wanted to shoot at.

The first deer was a doe. I made out her large, shadowy ears, and I marveled at how motionless these animals could hold themselves. She took one slow step forward. I saw her shoulder muscles ripple. She took another step. The animal behind her was a doe, also. Now the three deer moved together, in a series of hops, which made the tramping sound. They all had large mule ears, but as the third deer disappeared behind a pair of reddish-brown tree trunks, the sunlight glinted on a set of antlers.

My heartbeat jumped. It was like Grandpa said. The buck doesn't lead the parade. He often lets the does go first, maybe even pushes them, and he hangs back to see if it's safe.

I took deliberate breaths to try to keep myself still, but my hands were trembling. I brought my rifle up and steadied myself against the trunk of the tree I stood behind. I eased a shell into the chamber and kept my finger off the trigger. I waited for the animals to appear on the left side of the trees they had gone behind.

A minute later, I saw a dark shape, a doe. It was not where I expected it. It had already moved along the shadowy trail, and I had not seen it. Now that I had them relocated, I lined up my sights and held steady as I waited for the other two to show. The second doe appeared, and I relaxed. I did not want to stay all tensed up. Then the buck poked his head forward. I saw his dark nose and the front part of his antlers, less than a hundred yards away. He took another step, and another. I saw the muscles flex on his front quarters, and I settled the bead into the notch.

I pulled the trigger, and the world seemed to fall apart as the explosion crashed and echoed. The buck lurched forward, first up, then with his head lowered as he plunged into the timber. The two does bounded away, crunching twigs and branches, until all went silent.

My heart was pounding, and my mouth was dry. I couldn't believe I missed him, but I had the greatest fear that he had gotten away.

I hurried toward the spot where he had stood. I was heedless of noise now, as I stepped on branches on the ground and snapped twigs off the logs I crawled over. First I found a spatter of blood on dry pine needles and dirt, then marks where his hooves had torn up the path as he bolted away. I followed the trail for about fifty yards until I found him lying on his side, still and dead.

I counted three tines on each side of his antlers. His sleek, muscled body had a coat of brownish grey, and bright red blood trickled from a small hole where the bullet had gone in. The realization was settling in that I had just killed a deer. All of my hunting had come to a stop.

Now I had to think of what to do next. I didn't have to worry about following a wounded deer and getting lost, but even at that, I felt alone in a big world all around me. I got hold of myself and reasoned out where I was.

I was in the middle of the woods on the ridge of the Osteen Breaks with a deer I had shot. My grandfather was a long ways in back of me, but I could find him, and he could tell me what to do. I began to walk away, then stopped, turned, and came back. I thought hard. I needed to leave some kind of a signal so I would know how to find my deer again.

Rummaging in my shirt and trouser pockets, I found a white handkerchief that I carried but hardly ever used. I shook it out and tied it to a low-hanging pine branch. Then I set off through the timber, headed toward my grandfather and the horses. Every once in a while, I turned back to catch sight of the handkerchief.

Grandpa came up with a plan to take the horses along the lower edge of the timber and keep pace with me as I retraced my way to the deer. Once the handkerchief came in sight, I forged ahead with more confidence, and when I arrived at the deer, I called out to Grandpa. He called back. I took off my jacket, laid it on a log, and went to work at dressing the deer as Grandpa had told me.

First I used my string to tie a leg up to a nearby sapling so that the midsection would be clear to work on. Cutting from the inside out, I opened the pale-colored underbelly from between the hind legs up to the dark chest. Reaching in, I trimmed the connecting tissue wherever the entrails were connected, and I cut away the diaphragm between the intestines and the heart and lungs. After reaching deep down and cutting the windpipe and the gullet, I pulled out the whole set of innards and rolled them in a heap onto the ground. I cut loose the liver and laid it in the cavity. Next, after turning over the purple, splotchy lungs, I slit the sac around the heart, cut it loose, and slipped it into the carcass with the liver.

All of this took about an hour, and much of the work was slippery and made me feel awkward, but I heeded Grandpa's advice and did not hurry on any part of it. When I was done, I wiped my hands on the grass so that at least my palms were clean.

I stood up and rested my back as I waited for the carcass to air out. After a few minutes, I bent to my work again and cut holes along each side of the big cut. I took down the string and used it to lace up the loose sides of the belly as I had been told much earlier.

At this point, the figure of a person appeared to my left, coming from the direction I had come. Within a few seconds, I recognized Jeff Hayden, jumping up on large fallen logs and jumping over the more low-lying ones. He was carrying a rifle, and he had a smile on his face.

"You look like you could use some help," he said as he came within ten yards.

I stood up straight and took a deep breath. I had tied my hair back in the morning, but wisps and strands of it had come loose. My hands and forearms were bloody up to my elbows, and I had gooey blood on the backs of my fingers, so I couldn't brush my hair out of the way. I blew at it as I frowned at Jeff Hayden. "I'll do all right by myself," I said.

He stepped up onto a log and jumped down with both feet together. "Big deer, little girl."

I ignored him as I walked over to my jacket and took a rope out of the back pouch. It was a thirty-foot, half-inch hemp rope that Grandpa had taken from the pack equipment and lent to me for dragging the deer. He told me not to cut it because he wanted to use it later for tying the deer onto the horse. I bent over and began to wrap the rope around the neck of the dressed animal.

Without a word, Jeff moved in close to me, his hip against mine, and laid his hands on the rope. To do so, he stuck his right arm between my left arm and my chest, and he reached his left arm around the other side of mine. In a few seconds, he tied a slipknot and pulled the rope tight under the buck's jaws and ears. I didn't like him taking that liberty with my deer, but it didn't end there. As he backed away and stood up, he rubbed his right arm against my chest.

Dread ran through me. I drew my elbows against my ribs and stepped away from him. "I don't like you touching me," I said.

"I didn't mean nothin' by it."

"I don't care. I don't like it. I don't even like you interfering with my deer."

He wore a half-smile as he stared at me. "You know, I kind of like it when you get mad. Goes with your red hair."

"My hair isn't red. It's auburn."

"Looks red to me." His eyes traveled over me. "I like red-haired girls. We'd make a good pair."

"No, we wouldn't." I looked for as many points of difference as I could find in those few seconds. I noted that his eyes were blue, and mine were green. I despised his pale complexion, his upturned nose, even his superior height. I huffed out a breath. "I wish you would leave. I don't want to have to call my grandpa."

"Huh. You do get mad. But that's all right. I'll leave." He turned away, picked up his rifle where he had left it, skipped over a log, and headed back in the direction he had come.

I could feel that my pressure inside had gone up, and my mouth was dry. The blood on my forearms and the backs of my hands had dried tight, so I moved my hands to loosen them. I leaned over my deer again, untied Jeff Hayden's knot, and re-tied the rope into a bowline like Grandpa had taught me. I didn't care if it took me the rest of the day. I was going to drag this deer by myself.

I held the rope around the back of my waist, leaned into it, and pulled as I stepped backward. The antlered head came up, and the body inched forward. I looked around. Jeff Hayden was long gone, and I was glad of it.

I knew it would be difficult to tell anyone about what had happened. People might say, "It was just a boy getting too close. You know how clumsy they are." Or, "He didn't mean anything by it. It might have been an accident."

But I knew it wasn't. I also knew he didn't do it because I was pretty. He did it because I was a girl and he had the chance to do it. It made me as sick as if I had smelled a snake.

As for boys, I remember thinking that day that I didn't feel one way or another about them. Maybe someday I would meet a fella and want to get to know him better, but I wasn't certain. I just knew that I didn't like this one boy or anything he had in mind.

In camp that evening, after a supper of deer tenderloin fried in bacon grease, I washed the dishes and wiped out the cast-iron skillet. Grandpa was lying on top of his bed, still dressed, with a grey wool blanket pulled up to his chest. He had his hands folded and resting on the blanket. It had been a long day for him, hobbling around doing everything the hard way.

His eyes were closed, but every once in a while he would open them. When he saw me looking at him, he smiled.

"You did well, Katie. We've got deer meat to eat, and a pretty set of antlers."

I recalled an image of the deer slung over the saddle, tied snug, with his antlered head lashed to the saddle horn. It was a sight I would remember for a long time. I said, "I wouldn't have known how to do any of it without you, Grandpa."

"Well, we git along all right. Some kids, you take 'em out, and the next thing you know, they're tellin' you how to hunt."

I thought of the deer hanging in the tree near our camp. "We've got a lot of work to do tomorrow, getting packed and loaded up."

"Oh, yeah." Grandpa closed his eyes and fell into a light sleep again.

I looked at him as I sometimes did, and I thought, this is my mother's father. There was a time not long ago when I never knew him, and now it seemed as if I had known him forever. I could not remember a time earlier when someone loved me, but now I knew what it was like to love and be loved. There was nothing else like it, and I was glad to have it for as long as it would last.

★ ★ ★ ★ ★

MAN OF TREES

★ ★ ★ ★ ★

Case was watering his small cedar trees with a pair of tin buckets when an old man came shuffling down the lane. The stranger wore loose-fitting clothes and had a blanket roll slung over his shoulder. He was moving slow. Case pumped two more buckets of water as the man made his way to the yard. The dragging steps came to a halt, and the traveler raised his hand to shade his eyes.

"Afternoon," he said.

"And good afternoon to you. Can I offer you a drink of water?"

"In a little while. I need to catch my breath." The old man's posture had sagged when he stopped, and now he was taking slow breaths with his mouth open.

"Where are you headed?"

"Wyoming."

"You're in Wyoming."

"I know." The old man's gaze did not seem to settle on anything in particular as his chest went up and down.

Case did not sense any danger about the man. He felt sympathy, but he knew he should use caution with drifting strangers. The man was below average height and did not wear a hat. He had thinning grey hair, a weathered face, and greying stubble. He wore dirty, ragged clothing that hung upon him. His shirt was open all the way down the front, showing dirt on his wrinkled neck and meager chest. Case grimaced. He had not seen dirt caked like that on a person, but he held his judgment. The man did not look well.

The tired eyes rose. "I was wonderin' if you could spare a bite to eat. I'll work for it."

"I suppose so. Would you like some food now?"

"Oh, no. I'll do my work. Then I'll eat." He slipped the bundle from his shoulder and let it lie on the ground. The frayed blankets were tied with a length of quarter-inch rope, which, like the man's blankets and clothes, might well have had a previous owner.

"Have a drink, then, and I'll see what kind of work I can find."

"Huh?"

Case waved his hand at the two buckets. "Have a drink of water. Rinse your face if you'd like."

"Oh. Yeah." The old man bent over, then made a slow descent to one knee and drank from his cupped hands. He splashed water on his face and made a sputtering sound as he pushed himself up.

Case led the way, and the visitor followed at his elbow, taking uneven steps. "Here's a little plot of trees I have. These are elm. I dig them up wherever I find them, volunteers, and I put them here where I can tend to them. After a year or two, when they grow knee-high or taller, I sell them."

"Oh, that's good."

"Right now, they need weeding. I'll get you a knife for the ones that don't pull easy."

"That'll be fine."

"What's your name, by the way?"

"Hobson. Bill Hobson."

"My name's Case. Bob Case, but everyone just calls me by my last name."

Hobson lowered himself to the ground and went to work

picking at weeds with one hand as he leaned on the other. Case brought him the weeding knife and left him to his work.

Case resumed watering the cedar trees. The weather was not hot, as the season had moved into early fall, but Case wanted to give all of his trees a final watering before he let them draw into themselves for winter.

When he finished with the cedars, Case thought he should check on his worker. He was afraid he might find Hobson keeled over, mashing one or more little elm trees, but he found the old man still on his knees, leaning on one hand, poking at the dirt with the knife. He had taken out very few weeds in half an hour, and he was not leaving a clean area.

Case spoke in a raised voice. "It's about mealtime, I think."

Hobson turned his head to look up. "Is it?"

"I think so."

Inside the homesteader shack, Hobson rested in a chair as Case cooked up some deer meat and potatoes. The old man had a blank expression on his face and did not seem to be in a hurry for anything.

Case spoke above the crackling of the frying pan. "First deer of the season."

"Oh, that's the best."

Case served Hobson a medium-sized portion and a similar amount for himself. As he dug into his own meal, he saw that Hobson ate very little. He poked at his food and pushed it around, took a bite now and then, and chewed it in slow movements.

Case finished his first serving, and seeing that his guest would not want more, he served himself the rest. When he had his plate cleaned, he said, "Is the food all right, friend?"

"Oh, yes," said Hobson. "Just fine. But I can't eat much at a time. My body doesn't work the way it used to."

"Well, take your time. There's no hurry."

Hobson stared at his plate. Without looking up, he said, "I haven't had a drink in a long time, but I think one would help me eat."

The old man's comment made sense. Although his face was not flushed or swollen as Case had seen in some people whom he interpreted as being pickled, Hobson had some of the slow and blurred mannerisms that Case recognized as the long-term effects of drinking.

"Oh," said Case.

"I didn't mean to—"

"That's all right. I'll see if I can find something." Case went to the cupboard, took down the whiskey bottle, and poured two fingers in a glass. He handed it to Hobson and poured a smaller amount for himself.

Hobson nibbled at his drink, took a sip, then a larger sip, and had the whole thing down the hatch within a couple of minutes. "That helps," he said. He pulled his plate close and took a couple of more bites.

When it looked as if the old man had eaten all he was going to, Case cleared the plates and made ready to clean up.

Hobson said, "I know I didn't do much work, but the food and drink did me a lot of good." He had his gaze resting on the empty glass, which sat a few inches from his hand.

"I'd be glad to pour you another one if you don't think it'll do any harm."

"Not at all. Thank you. That's very generous." Hobson raised his eyes and smiled.

The old man stirred in his blankets on the floor the next morning. Case was glad to see the movement, for it dispelled his fear that his guest would die in the night. As Hobson sat up and rubbed his eyes, Case spoke to him.

"And how are you this morning?"

"Mighty fine. Couldn't be better."

"Do you think you could take on some breakfast?"

"Oh, I don't think so. As a general rule, I don't eat this early in the day."

"A cup of coffee?"

"Not quite yet."

Hobson fussed around with his blankets and few belongings, and in a short while he had his bundle rolled up and tied. He stood up and blinked his eyes. "I think I'll be on my way," he said.

"So soon? The coffee's almost ready."

"No thanks. I'll get out of your way and let you have your breakfast."

"Are you sure?"

"Oh, yes. I like to get an early start." Hobson leaned over to pick up his bundle, and he pulled in a breath as he straightened up.

"I was going to offer to heat water for a bath. I've got a tub, and we can put it—"

Hobson waved his hand. "Not at all. I'm fine." He slipped the rope over his shoulder. "Thanks for everything. I hope the good Lord rewards you."

"I never expect a reward. I'm just glad to help."

"I know what you mean. Thanks again. I'll be on my way."

"Good luck."

The tinkling song of the meadowlark carried on the morning air, varying from five to seven notes. The sun cast its warmth on Case's left cheek as he stood on his ladder and reached for apples. His were small, light green apples with a blush of red, the kind that grew in this climate. In good years such as this, he could pick two or three at a time, holding a branch of dark green leaves with one hand, lifting each apple free, and letting it

drop into his canvas picking bag. The only sounds of the morning were the rustle of leaves, the faint thud of one apple upon
another, the creak of the ladder step, and the song of the
meadowlark.

He kept up a steady pace, for he wanted to have all of his
apples in when the ditch water came for the last watering of the
season. He tried to let the apples grow as long as he could, and
he kept an eye on the windfalls and bird pecks to have an idea
of how the apples were ripening. He could not go by the
calendar, as no two years were the same. As with so many
aspects of raising plants and gathering produce, both wild and
domestic, apple picking required a sense or feeling about when
to do things.

Still, it was not like pulling garlic. He had dug his about six
weeks earlier. He knew when to do it by the number of dry
leaves, but he had his first look at the crop when he pulled it
out of the moist, mulch-covered ground. At least he could watch
the apples all along.

His bag was almost half full when he stepped down from the
ladder, so he stooped to an empty bushel basket, loosened the
two rope catches, lowered the bottom of the bag to open it, and
let the apples go rumbling into the bushel. He reset his ladder
and climbed up, to begin at the top as usual. At this vantage
point, more than twelve feet off the ground, he enjoyed for a
few seconds his wide view of the countryside. Having moved
the ladder, and having regained his elevation, he saw things
anew.

He drew his brows together. Less than a quarter of a mile to
the east, where the road ran past the edge of his property, a human form lay in the shade of a small stand of chokecherry
bushes. Case knew those bushes, for he had gone there about a
month earlier and picked almost a bucket of the small, dark
fruit. Now the leaves were turning from green to yellow, pink,

and crimson. Some leaves had fallen, so the shade was not thick, but it was enough to offer a bit of comfort.

Case was sure that the human form was old Hobson, stretched out in his drab clothes. The man had said he liked to get an early start, but he hadn't walked much more than half a mile. Case felt a twinge of dread, as before, that the man might have lain down to die, but his worry vanished when the grey-haired figure raised up on one elbow, turned, and lay down again. Case took a breath of fresh air and continued his apple picking.

Case was emptying his bag into the third bushel of the morning when he saw a rider on horseback at the western edge of his property. He recognized the rider as Lum Woodhull. The man lived across the road and a ways north but had a pasture and a couple of alfalfa fields over on this side. Case felt a gnawing in his stomach, but he knew he needed to talk to the man, so he set out at a fast walk. He hollered once, twice. When the rider turned in the saddle, Case waved. The man on horseback waited.

Case had not taken the time to leave off his picking bag, so he still had it slung over his shoulder with his hand resting on the lip, a semicircle of stiff rope with the canvas hemmed over. He felt pedestrian, looking up at Lum, mounted on a shiny bay horse. The man's silvery hair, hawklike nose, and dark eyes were cast in the shadows of his dark hat as he looked down. Case stopped about five yards away, and Lum's voice came out sharp.

"Say, what do you want?"

"I need to talk to you."

"That's what you're doing."

Case drew a breath. "It's about the water."

"Water."

"Yes, the ditch water. My allotment isn't much, but I can't have you taking it. I have a right to it, and I need it to water my trees."

Lum moved his shoulder, as if he was twitching off a fly. "Of course you do. Who said I ever took any?"

Case had to pull himself together to speak back. "I know you've done it. In broad daylight as well as at night. You open your headgate and close off someone else's, and then you come back and change it, and the other person gets hardly any of his own water."

Lum swung down from his horse and took a couple of steps forward. He passed his reins to his left hand and had his six-gun and holster in plain view. Small flecks of spit flew as he spoke. "Are you saying I steal?"

Case felt himself backing up, though he stood still. "What I'm saying is that I have a right to my water, like anyone does."

Lum scowled. "And I've got a right to mine. I would never do such a thing as steal someone else's." His chest went up. "And I don't let little scrubs like you push me around by saying I did." He turned his back on Case, put his spurred boot in the stirrup, and stepped up into the saddle. As he reined around, he stopped to bear down on his neighbor. "Anything else? I've got work to do back home, but I came over here to see if anyone had cut into my ditch."

Case shook his head. He was sure Lum was making up the last part, to go along with his bald-faced lie. But he had no answer.

Swallows were flitting back and forth in the barnyard, and the shadows of evening had grown long enough to touch the whitewashed house. Case dismounted from his horse as the chorus of chicken cackles died down. He stood for a moment before tying the horse to the hitching rail. The tall, solid form of Jerome Fairfax was moving from the barn to the house, leaning forward and taking heavy steps.

The older man did not pay Case much attention as he passed

by and said, "Evenin'.""

"Good evening, Mr. Fairfax."

"Cecile's about."

"Very good. Thanks."

Case tied the brown horse and waited. High above, a nightjar made its curious honking song. Like the swallows, it was catching food on the wing.

Here at ground level, the air was dry and dusty. Case had perspired a little on his ride, but he was glad he had found time for a bath before he left.

Cecile's light-colored figure appeared from around the corner of the house. "Hello-o."

"Hello to you," he said.

Her smile was visible as she approached, and he smiled in return. She did not walk fast. She was not coy or teasing, as he had come to know her, but shy, and in a country way, coquettish. Her wavy dark hair hung to her shoulders and below, framing her rounded cheekbones and tanned complexion. She had blackcherry eyes and prominent teeth, all to a pleasant effect. She wore a light blue dress he had seen before, buttoned at the neck and covering her ankles. It showed her to be as tall as she was, which was about an inch taller than Case.

She held out her hand, quite cordial, and he took it. "I was hoping you would visit."

"I'm glad to be able to." He caught a trace of bath soap, and he appreciated that she might have taken a bath when she changed out of the clothes she wore for tending sheep.

"And how is the man of trees?"

"Quite well. And the shepherdess of the valley?"

"Also well." She smiled. "And your work?"

"Picking apples. I hope to finish in time for the ditch water."

"Oh, yes."

"I thought I might bring you some before long. Apples, not

ditch water. Give me a reason to visit again and work my way into the good graces of your parents."

She laughed. "Every bit helps."

He did not have to say more. They had a good understanding, which he carried with him. In the two years he had been paying his visits, he had learned that for many years her parents had hoped to marry her off so they would not have to support her forever. But she was good at farm and domestic work, and with age creeping up on the parents, they had arrived at a point where they would rather she not marry but stay home and take care of things. They had even told her that a man did not want to marry a woman who was taller or superior in any way. When she told Case, they both laughed. And shared a little kiss. By his calculation, she was six years younger than he was. He had marked forty a year earlier. He saw her as fresh and unblemished.

"Anything new?" he asked.

"I worked on a poem today. You know, I carry a little notebook and pencil with me, and when a line occurs to me, I write it down."

"I remember you mentioned it before. It seems—well, poetic."

"Papa doesn't see much value in it, but I don't see any harm in trying to write a sonnet."

"I wouldn't think so." He had heard her recite verses from other poets, but she had not shared any of her own, either recited or written. He thought she was rather modest, or at least reserved, about it.

"And yourself? Any news?"

"Other than picking apples—well, I had a run-in with Lum Woodhull."

"Whatever for?"

"I had to tell him I didn't want him to be taking my water. I don't get much, and I need it for my trees. Of course, he said he would never do such a thing. But I know he does."

"Of course he does. And he steals water from others as well. He takes water that Papa is supposed to have for his corn. And just as he does with you, he denies it."

"At least I mentioned it to him."

"And well you did. If more people say something to his face, it might help him realize what it looks like."

"You would hope so, but some people don't have much shame."

"That's true. As I read once, it is much better if we all tend to our own gardens."

The silver tune of the meadowlark had subsided, and the morning air was beginning to warm. In the quiet world of his little orchard, Case could hear the apples rub against the inside of the canvas picking bag as he shifted on the ladder. The *hoo-hoo* of a mourning dove carried on the air, followed by the flapping of wings. Silence resumed, but a moment later it gave way to the tread of footsteps.

Case dropped two more apples into the bag and made his way down the ladder. He recognized his visitor as Luther Mark, who would have come across a few fields. Case bent over, pulled the knotted ropes from the flat metal hooks, and let the apples tumble into the bushel basket. As he waited, he tucked the short ropes back into place.

Mark was moving at a fast pigeon-toed walk, and his hand raised in a rapid back-and-forth wave. His ears stuck out beneath his cloth cap, his spectacles glinted, and his small tuft of beard moved from side to side, as if he was rehearsing his delivery. When he came to a stop, breathing hard, he blurted out, "Man's been found dead."

"Where?"

"Up by Lanyi's."

61

"That's too bad. Anyone we know?" As Case spoke, he placed the Lanyi homestead, about a mile north and on the same side of the road as his own place.

"Stranger."

"Old, young?"

"Old man. Looked like a hobo."

"Oh, my. I think I might have known him. A grimy old man, with nothing but a bedroll of shabby blankets."

"That's him."

"He stayed over at my place, night before last." Case let the news sink in. "I'm sorry to hear it, but I can't say I'm surprised. He didn't seem as if he had much left in him."

Mark's dull blue eyes grew wide. "It didn't look like he went in peace. He had great big purple bruises on his throat. Someone choked him."

"Are you sure? When I saw him, he had a dark layer of dirt on his throat."

"He still had some of that, but some of it was rubbed off. These were bruises, all right. You could almost see the thumb marks."

Case swallowed with difficulty. "That's terrible. I wonder why someone would want to do that. He seemed like an innocent old man to me."

"Some people just have it in 'em. Hotheaded. They think the Bohunk did it."

A picture rose in Case's mind of Lanyi, the one they called the Bohunk—dark-haired, dark-eyed, swarthy, muscular, always dressed in field clothes. He spoke with an accent, and he could have been from any of several countries that people in this part of the country lumped together as a combination of Bohemia and Hungary. Case had heard of other individual places, such as Bulgaria, Romania, and Serbia, but he was not sure he could find them on a map. Still, he did not refer to the volatile neighbor as others did.

"What reason would Lanyi have?" he asked.

"Might not take much. You know how he is. They're a wild bunch, him and his woman and their kids."

Case had a less distinct image of Mrs. Lanyi, as he had not seen much of her. He understood that she was a cross between Indian and Negro, and the three children were dark. People said that the oldest, a girl, was hers from before she knew Lanyi.

Case said, "I don't know any of them very well, but it doesn't seem fair to accuse someone without any reason."

"Well, he swears he doesn't know a thing about it. And he hasn't been arrested or anything."

"That's not so bad. But they still suspect him. And I'm sorry to hear about the old man. He said his name was Hobson, by the way. He wasn't doing any harm to anyone. But if someone did him in, there had to be a reason."

"Like I say, it might not take much." Mark's dull blue eyes moved from side to side. "Looks like you've got work to do. I won't keep you from it."

"I'm hoping to get the rest of these picked today, before the water comes. Thanks for sharing the news, though I'm sorry to hear it."

"That's the way news is, most of the time." Mark's eyes flickered. "Well, I'd better be going." He turned and pushed off to the south at a fast, uneven gait.

Case headed toward his ladder. As he set his foot on the first step, he paused and faced north. He remembered Hobson's smile when he accepted the second drink of whiskey. "So long, friend. I'm sorry you didn't get to live a little longer."

Case had a good store of apples in his lean-to, where he also had his garlic hanging and his pumpkins stacked. His last bushel was not quite full, and he had a plan for that amount.

He divided it into two panniers on the packsaddle of his white donkey, and mounting the brown horse, he set out for the Fairfax homestead.

The chickens met him with their usual cackle. Jerome Fairfax came out from the back door of the house, curved-stem pipe in hand, and cast an appraising look at the pack animal.

"What have you got there?"

"Some apples, sir." Case dismounted.

"That looks like quite a bit."

He had said the same thing the year before. Case, undaunted, gave a similar answer now. "There's enough for several pies, and plenty for drying. Some people buy a whole bushel just to cut and dry and put away."

Mr. Fairfax puffed on his pipe. "I suppose so. Let's put them in the barn until we can get to them."

Case tied the horse and led the donkey across the yard. In the fading light inside the barn, he transferred the apples a double handful at a time into the open mouth of a burlap sack, held by Cecile's father. When the two bulging sacks were resting against the wooden grain bin, Case took a plump apple and put it in his vest pocket.

"Thanks," said the older man.

Case detected a reserved note, not quite grudging, from the man who recognized that he might be losing his daughter. "You're welcome," he said.

Case led the donkey out into the yard, where the twilight lingered. Cecile appeared, wearing a dove-colored dress in the same style as the one she had worn the evening before. Case understood that she sewed her dresses herself, and although she did not have the figure of an eighteen-year-old girl, she did not do hers an injustice.

Her smile showed, and she spoke. "How do you do? Thank you for the apples."

"A small token." He came to a stop.

She petted the donkey on the nose, then rubbed her knuckles on his forehead. "How's Jig?"

"He's doing well. Happy to bring you the tribute."

She smiled again, with a gleam of white.

He took out the apple along with his pocketknife, opened the knife, and cut the apple in two. He handed the good half to her and cut out the small worm hole on his half.

She took a bite, chewed, and swallowed. "Very good. These apples have real taste."

"They do."

"Tart but not sour. I don't know why people prefer the type that is all water and sugar."

"More luxury. But these are the kind that grow here." Before he took a bite, he said, "I suppose you heard the news."

"About the old man they found? It was very sad."

"Yes. I believe he's the one who spent the night at my place."

"That's what neighbor Mark said. My father talked to some others as well."

"Oh. Are there any suspects? Mark said the suspicion fell on Lanyi, but with nothing in particular."

"That's what Papa said. The Lanyis had no motive. The old man did not stop at their place, and Mr. Lanyi has declared that they never so much as saw him."

"People seem to be ready to say something unkind anyway, about Lanyi, his wife, or the children."

"Yes, they do. But they work hard like anyone else. Mr. Lanyi works from dawn to dusk in his fields, and even the children work. Lum Woodhull pays or has paid the two older ones a pittance to break up branches for kindling from a tree that blew over last winter."

"Lum," he said.

"Yes. It's short for Columbus, you know."

"No, I didn't."

"The poem is very famous."

"I remember it from school."

Her eyes took on a shine as she recited the first stanza.

> Behind him lay the gray Azores,
> Behind the Gates of Hercules;
> Before him not the ghost of shores,
> Before him only shoreless seas.

"That's the poet's touch," she said. "In school, he's always a hero. In reality, I imagine he was like the other explorers."

"Like Lum himself. Takes what he can get. I hope I don't have any trouble with him over this last share of water."

"I hope not, also, but he gives people reason to be apprehensive."

Case enjoyed the quiet before dawn as he drank a cup of coffee. He had been told to expect the water at about two in the morning, and he had stood in the moonlight with his shovel at hand as the first shallow flood came flowing down the ditch. The head of water, as the ditch men called it, was never great, but it reached its full flow in about ten minutes. He was to receive his water for six hours, then close his headgate and open the gate that would allow the water to flow down the ditch to the next user. When he was satisfied that his share was flowing into his parcel, he went home.

He estimated that three hours had passed. He blew out the lamp, found his shovel in the lean-to, and walked out into the dim moonlight. Following his usual practice, he headed for the far end of his orchard. He would walk back up through the middle and see how far the water had traveled.

The ground at the far end was dry, which he considered normal. Sometimes the fringe of water reached that far in the first three hours, and sometimes it did not. He walked toward the source, crossing back and forth between tree rows, and the ground underfoot continued to crunch. He did not find damp ground until he came within twenty yards of the source, and even at that, no water showed. He stepped up onto the ditch bank and saw nothing in the ditch bottom but mud. To be sure, he leaned over and poked the tip of his shovel into the sludge.

A picture of Lum Woodhull rose in his mind. This was Lum's trick—to lie in wait, steal over half the allotted time, and turn the water back in.

First daylight was showing as Case walked along the ditch bank. Thinking of a good approach, he rested the point of his shovel head in the ditch bottom and vaulted across to the other side. He stepped down to the other side, leaned over, and continued on his way. From time to time, he looked up to see how close he was coming to Lum's alfalfa field.

When he reached the headgate that controlled the water in the ditch, he stopped. He knew how it was built—a wooden box set into the ditch, with a slot going down each side. Upright boards, one on top of the other, fitted into the slots to regulate or stop the flow. The gate was about a yard across. Case had stepped across this one and others many times in the daylight. At the moment, water gleamed in the full ditch on the upstream side of the gate, while the ditch bottom on the left side was a dark shine of mud.

Holding his shovel crosswise, Case climbed up the ditch bank, paused, and planted his foot in preparation for the step across. He moved a couple of inches to the left and settled his foot again. As he stepped forward, the dark form of Lum Woodhull lunged up from the other side, the glow of a cigarette burning in the middle of his face. Lum raised his shovel, swung, and struck a blow on Case's right shoulder.

Case lost all balance. The best he could do was to keep his

shovel head clear of his face and to take the fall on his left shoulder and hip. He hit the mud all along the left side of his body, and he felt the smear of it on his face and in his eye.

Lum's voice rang out in a vaunting tone. "No son of a bitch comes sneaking up on me, by God! Ha-ha! You look like a carp that's been layin' in the mud."

Case rose to his elbow, found his hat, and stood up. He leaned on his shovel to keep from slipping in the mud. "No shame," he said. "Stealing water, and caught in the act."

"I'm taking what I deserve. There's enough for you. Here." Lum bent over and pulled out the top board, and water began spilling into the ditch at Case's feet. Lum caught at the second board with the corner of his shovel and wobbled that board out as well.

Case climbed out of the ditch on his hands and knees with the shovel in front of him. "There's nothing funny about this. You're going to hear about it. Caught in the act."

Lum's voice turned menacing. "You're damn right there's nothing funny. You're just lucky I didn't fetch you one in the head. I wish I had."

Case felt a chill run through him. He could not see if Lum was carrying a pistol, but he thought he had better not provoke him any more. With his shovel at his side, he trudged back toward his own parcel. Lum had pulled out the third board, and the full head of water was on its way.

Case was still feeling agitated by midmorning. He had gotten a minimal irrigation for his trees and had passed the water on, and he had cleaned up at home. The rest of the day lay ahead of him, but he could not sit still and plan his work. Something in Lum Woodhull's manner was not right. The man was shameless about stealing water and being caught at it, and yet he had sounded like he meant it when he said he wished he had hit

Case in the head.

Case closed his eyes and opened them. Breaking up his sleep made for a long day. He should take a nap. He had his apples in and his last watering done. But something ate on him. He was going to have to go out and see what he could learn.

The Lanyi residence was about the same size as many of the homesteader shacks, perhaps sixteen feet square, and from its appearance, it was homemade and not a package model. A few brown and white chickens scratched in the yard, and a tan goat grazed at the end of a stake rope. The goat stared and made a *"beh-heh-heh"* sound as Case dismounted from his horse.

As he had not come this close to the house before, he now noted its split lumber, flaking paint, and general uncleanliness. He had seen others more squalid, and he knew that making a living on a homestead was far from easy for a man with a family. He hoped Lanyi had come in from the fields for noon dinner. Case was satisfied that he had guessed right when the man appeared in the open doorway. He had his sleeves rolled up, showing pale forearms in contrast with his hands and face.

"Are you Mr. Lanyi?"

"Ya-ya. What do you want?"

"I'm sorry to interrupt your dinner if I am, but I'd like to ask some questions."

The man had taken off his hat. His dark hair stood out where it had not been matted down, and his dark eyes held on his visitor. "Everybody asks questions. We don't know nothing."

"I know. And I don't want to trouble you. But I understand that your children have been working for Lum Woodhull."

"Oh, him. The penny-pincher."

"I was wondering if your children saw anything while they were working there."

"If they saw what?"

Case spoke in clear syllables. "This is just an idea, but I think the old man might have gone by that way. The old man who died. He stayed one night at my place, and when he moved on, he went in that direction."

"Wal, he never came by here."

"But he might have gone by there, you see?"

"Hah. We ask the kids." Lanyi turned to face the interior of the house and hollered, "Marika, Rudy. Come here."

A minute later, Lanyi pushed two dark children in front of him. The boy was about eight years old, and the girl was about eleven or twelve. A smaller child stood in back of the father, looking out.

Lanyi said, "This man wants to know what you seen at Lum's."

The boy's eyes were fixed at the level of Case's knees, while the girl's eyes moved from Case to the horse and back.

"When you were working for Lum," Case said. "Especially the day before yesterday."

The girl made a kind of pout and shook her head.

"Tell him," said Lanyi. "Tell him the truth." Lanyi spoke in a sharp voice, and both children seemed to shrink at it.

The girl scratched behind her ear. "Nothing. We just worked. We broke sticks."

"The day before yesterday," Case prompted.

Lanyi said, "That's the day Rudy got the bellyache, wasn't it?" The girl looked up at him as if she had been hit in the past but knew how to take it. "Tell him," said the father. He pushed her half a step toward Case.

The girl was wearing a plain cotton dress the color of charcoal. Her straight, dark hair hung to her shoulders, and her bare feet showed below the dress. She did not look straight at Case, but she spoke.

"That was the day. We broke sticks in the morning, and we

came home to eat. Rudy got sick, so I went back and worked by myself."

Case felt a twinge of discomfort, but he kept a cheerful tone. "What's your name?"

"Marika."

"That's a nice name. Now tell me, when you were working there that day, either in the morning or in the afternoon, did an old man come by?"

Marika nodded.

"An old man with no hat and a roll of blankets hanging from his shoulder?"

Marika nodded again.

"Did he say anything? Did he stop and talk to Lum?"

"He asked for something to eat, and Lum told him to go away."

"Was that all they said?"

The girl did not speak.

"Tell him," said Lanyi.

"He asked Lum if I was his daughter, and Lum said no."

Case felt set back for a second. "Anything else?"

Marika shook her head.

"Nothing else happened?"

"No."

"Was that the last day you worked for Lum?"

"Yes. He told me we didn't have to come back."

Lanyi said, "Lum still owes 'em the money. Should be about a dollar, but we'll see."

Case observed the girl. She was staring at the dirt with her lips pressed together.

"I guess that's it," said Lanyi. "You're the one with the trees, huh?"

"That's right."

Marika slipped inside, and Rudy followed.

71

Lanyi said, "Everything's a lotta work."

"It sure is. Well, thanks. And good luck."

"You velkum. And good luck with your trees."

The long shadows of evening stretched out on the east side of the house and lean-to. Case pushed hard with the rasp and ground off crumbs of dry bark from the stick he held against his knee. He gave some thought to his work. He had salvaged the piece of wood from an ash tree that had died in town. At six feet long and two inches thick, it was the size of a cudgel, but he was trimming it down. Ash was harder than elm or choke-cherry, so it made a good handle for an ax, a hoe, or a shovel. At present he had a walking stick in mind. But the work was slow, and Case had to stop every few minutes to flex his hand.

He looked up at the small grove of elms he had planted for shade. Three feet tall and fifteen feet apart, the little trees gave a suggestion of what they would grow into. He would like to try ash trees as well, but they took more care and more water. He needed to develop a plan for bringing ditch water up to this higher ground.

He went back to rasping the bark. He knew better than to try to hurry the job. If he worked on it a little bit at a time, he would get it shaped. Tomorrow he could go back to his regular work—put the panniers on the crossbuck and take some apples to town.

Movement at the corner of his eye caused him to look up again. A person had stepped out from the northeast corner of the house and stood in the shadow. Case was sure it was Lum Woodhull, but the man seemed out of place, as he rode his horse wherever he went and would have come up the front way.

Case spoke in a clear voice. "What is it?"

Lum took a couple of slow steps. "Come to pay you a visit."

Case shifted in his seat. Out of a sense of caution, he laid the rasp on the ground but kept hold of the stick as he stood up. "Do you have something you want to talk about?" Case thought that the incident with the ditch water was over, but he remembered how enraged Lum had become, and he did not know how strong a tendency the man might have to want to get even.

"You might say so." Lum took three more steps and made a quarter-turn as he came to a stop about ten feet away. He was wearing his gun and holster, as usual.

Case thought the man was making an effort to be reserved, but he did not think Lum had come to make amends. "Well, go ahead."

"I heard you been snoopin'." Lum seemed agitated, as his upper body did not keep still, and his hand moved.

Case had a flash memory of the visit with the Lanyis. Several hours had passed, and gossip could have gone back and forth among various neighbors. "Just a visit," he said.

Lum's voice took on a snarl as he said, "Well, I don't like it." He pulled his pistol in a jerky motion and fired a shot, which tore past Case's shoulder and made a *spang*! as it put a hole in the washtub hanging on the wall.

Case's heart was pounding. This man wanted to shoot him down, right here in his lean-to with his harvest at hand. Case had hold of his stick, but he didn't know which way to move.

Lum tried to steady the gun, but the tip of it wavered. His hand jerked, and the pistol made a *click*! His hand jerked again, but the gun remained silent. "Damn!" he barked, and he threw the pistol at Case.

Case dodged and made a break to the right, but Lum sprang at him, caught him by the arm, and pulled him off-balance. Case lost hold of the stick and tried to swing his fist, but Lum closed in on him and drove him to the ground. Lum straddled him, put a knee on his shoulder, and settled his hands on Case's neck.

The world closed in. Case felt the pressure, and his fear gave him a surge of strength. He bucked and thrashed and pushed Lum to the side, then scrambled to all fours. He couldn't let the man get on top of him again. Lum was larger and heavier, and he was strong.

Lum kicked him in the side of his chest as he was rising, but the boot glanced off. Case stood up and swung his fist, but Lum blocked it and drove a punch into Case's cheekbone.

Case staggered back and bent over, trying to keep himself from falling. Lum tried to kick him again, but he had to aim too high, and Case caught the boot and twisted it. The big man fell back.

Keeping his balance, Case reached for his stick where it had fallen. He took it with both hands and came up and around as the other man lunged at him. Case swung and caught Lum on the side of the head, and the man plunged forward.

Dusk was gathering as Case pulled his senses together. His hand was shaking, and his throat was dry. Somewhere a horse whinnied—Lum's, he imagined. The man at his feet did not move. Case knelt and laid a finger on the man's neck. He felt a pulse and let out a long breath of relief.

Case was cleaning up after the midday meal when the sound of hooves on dry ground brought him to the doorway. A buckboard was coming down the lane. Jerome Fairfax was handling the reins, and Cecile was sitting next to him on the bench with her hands in her lap. She raised a hand and waved. Case returned the greeting.

He had not put on his hat, so he stood in the shade of the lean-to and rolled down his sleeves. Mr. Fairfax brought the horses to a stop, tied the reins to the dashboard, and climbed down. He walked around and helped his daughter to the ground. She reached into the buckboard and took out a circular object with a golden-brown crust.

Case's interest increased. "What have we here?"

"A pie," she said, with a wide smile. "From your very own apples."

"How generous. Thank you." He nodded to her father and said, "Good afternoon."

"Same to you."

Cecile handed Case the pie. "I made two, so this one is all for you."

"Thanks again. Let me put it inside and lay a cloth over it. I'd invite you inside, but the shade is more comfortable out here."

"We'll wait," said the father.

When Case rejoined them, Cecile spoke first. "We heard about the incident, of course, and we were very glad to know that you weren't hurt. We heard he tried to shoot you."

"He did, but he was able to take only one shot, and not a good one, before his gun misfired and jammed. He got in a few licks by hand and foot before it was over, though." Case touched the swollen spot on his left cheekbone, which he knew had darkened.

Her father spoke in his serious tone but not quite so gruff as usual. "We're glad you were able to do what you did. He can face the law now."

Case glanced at the stick where it leaned against the wall, next to the perforated washtub. "I had some help, but I figured all was fair at that point. I don't suppose he's confessed to anything yet."

"No," said, Mr. Fairfax, "but it seems that they've gotten the Lanyi girl to tell more."

"Oh."

Fairfax glanced at his daughter and said, "It's not for polite company, but everyone will have heard it before long, anyway."

"I already have," said Cecile, "so you can tell him in front of me. I'm not a wilting flower, you know."

Fairfax acted as if she had not said anything or was quite present. He cleared his throat and said, "It seems that Lum did something he shouldn't have. The girl was working by herself in the afternoon, and Lum took to telling her that she was too dirty, and he made her take a bath in the water trough. The old man came by and asked for a meal, and Lum told him to be on his way. But the old man must have seen that something wasn't right, for the girl had had to take off some of her clothes, so he asked Lum if she was his daughter. Lum told him it was none of his business, and the old man said he ought not to be doing something like that with a girl who wasn't his daughter, that people would find out and do something. Lum blew up and cursed at the man, and when he was gone, Lum told the girl to go home. He also told her not to tell anyone about what happened."

"So we are left to imagine that Lum tracked the old man down and decided to keep him silent."

"That's the general assumption."

"He's got plenty to answer to, then."

"He does indeed. He wasn't very popular before. Even then, you might have found a dozen men who would stand in line for the privilege of knocking him on the head."

Case said, "It may have been a privilege, but I worked hard for it. He had me down at one point."

Cecile was beaming. She took a step toward the stick and held her hand, palm up, in its direction. "Is this it?"

"Yes, it is. I was planning to trim it down to a walking stick, but as you can see, it still had some heft when I was called upon to use it."

"A walking stick?"

"Yes. For snakes and such. But now that I think of it, when I have it trimmed, I could offer it to you as a staff for tending sheep. It wouldn't have a crook, though."

"A staff." She turned to him and kissed him on the forehead. "That would be lovely."

★ ★ ★ ★ ★

Night Horse

★ ★ ★ ★ ★

Finley Cole kept a night horse in the barn for all the time that I worked for him. He didn't keep the horse saddled, as some men did, but he had it in a stall so he wouldn't have to go out and catch one if something came up in the night. He had three or four horses that he rotated, depending on how much work they were getting otherwise, so that he wouldn't have the same one penned up every night. One of my jobs was to clean the stall each day and to have it ready for that evening's horse.

On one afternoon in late August, a stranger dropped by when I was cleaning the pen. He tied his horse outside and stood in the doorway. I didn't like looking at him with the bright light in back of him, so I told him to come in.

He was a normal-looking fellow in his mid-thirties, a little above average height, not decked out in gaudy clothes but not wearing rags, either. He was dressed like a range rider, with a dust-colored hat, a greyish-tan work shirt, a brown cloth vest, denim trousers, and boots with spurs.

"What can I help you with?" I asked.

"Does this place belong to Finn Cole?"

"It does."

"How long has he had it?"

"I don't know. I've been working here less than a year."

The stranger cast a glance around the inside of the barn. He had blue eyes, a clear complexion, and wavy brown hair. "How does he make a living?"

I thought the question was a bit personal, but I shrugged it off and said, "Like anyone else. Buys and sells cattle. Has cattle of his own but not a big range to graze 'em on. Buys and sells horses once in a while, as well."

"Does he have a fellow named Holbrook working for him?"

"Yes, he does. Ross Holbrook."

The stranger nodded. "And is there a woman named Evie Burns here?"

I looked at him straight and said, "I don't know how many of your questions I should answer."

He waved his hand. "That's all right."

I imagined he assumed that if Evie was not around, I would have said so. I narrowed my gaze on him and said, "What's your name, friend?"

"My name's Paul," he said. "Paul Pimentel."

"Good enough. Would you like me to tell Finn you were looking for him?"

"However you'd like. And your name?"

"Emerson Danforth," I said. "Everyone calls me Dan."

"That's good enough, too." He glanced around again and said, "I won't keep you from your work. Pleased to meet you."

"And the same here," I said.

The stranger wasn't gone long when Evie showed up. She was wearing an everyday dress of dark blue and had put on a light-colored straw hat with a wide brim and a round crown. Her dark brown hair fell to her shoulders, and her eyes, which varied in color, showed green. She had a worried expression on her face, and her hands worked together as if she was buttoning a shirt or winding a watch.

"Who was that man who stopped in?" she asked.

"He said his name was Paul Pimentel. He was asking about Finn."

Evie drew her brows together. "Was he asking to see him?"

"Not outright. He asked whether this was Finn's place, what he did for a living, if he had Ross Holbrook working here . . . and whether you were here."

Her face clouded. "I don't know why anyone would ask about me."

"Neither do I. And if it's any comfort, I didn't answer his question about you. That is, I told him I didn't know how many of his questions I should answer, but I think he would conclude that the reason I didn't answer was that you were here."

Her eyes met mine for a couple of seconds. "Thank you anyway." Her chest went up and down as she breathed, and with her eyes fixed at some point a few yards away, she said, "There was something familiar about that man, some sense I had, but I know I haven't seen him before."

"Well, he was a stranger to me. He seemed polite enough, even if he asked a lot of questions. Inquisitive, as my grandfather would say."

"Did he mention where he was from?"

"No. The only thing he said about himself was his name, and I had to ask for that. We might get a chance to know more about him, though. He didn't seem like he was going to leave right away."

She let out a short, weary breath. "I wouldn't expect anything good to come out of this."

"You never can tell," I said, but I knew I didn't have any wisdom to share. It was just something to say.

Finn came to the bunkhouse while Ross Holbrook and I were finishing breakfast the next morning. Holbrook and I were the only two living in the bunkhouse at the time, so Finn didn't mind much about what he said or how loud he said it.

"Some son of a bitch came by here yesterday afternoon."

Finn bored his brown eyes at me. "You talked to him, didn't you?"

"Not much," I said.

"Not much. Tell me what he said, or what he asked and what you told him."

I took a couple of seconds to pull my thoughts together. "Well, he asked if this was your place, how long you had it, what you did for a living, if Ross was working here, and if Evie was here. I gave short answers to all of the questions except the last one."

Finn scowled. "And you gave him a long answer to that one?"

"I didn't answer it."

"Well, saddle up. Both of you. We're going to town to have a talk with this bird. What did you say his name was?"

"He said it was Paul Pimentel."

As we rode into town, having covered the five miles in less than an hour, Holbrook pulled up next to Finn and asked, "How do you know he's here?"

Finn made a sound like "Puh" and said, "I just know things." He squared his shoulders, snorted, cleared his throat, and spit off to the side. He was a well-built fellow, of average height, and he carried himself straight up if he was in the saddle or on foot. I had never seen him tangle with anyone, but I had noticed that men did not crowd him.

We rode on without speaking. The three of us dismounted and tied up in front of the barbershop and post office. The barbershop was not open yet. Finn sent Holbrook into the post office to ask about the newcomer.

Holbrook came out a minute later. He took the toothpick from his mouth and rubbed his nose. "They said to try the café."

"Well, go ahead," said Finn.

The café was three doors down on our right, so Holbrook turned and strolled along the board sidewalk. He had something of a rolling gait, with his head tipped back and his arms swinging. He was heavier built than Finn, and he had an air about him that said that anyone who wanted to knock his hat off was welcome to give it a try.

Holbrook went into the café and came out a minute later. He stood on the sidewalk under the wooden awning and made a motion with his head. Finn and I walked in the street toward him.

As we drew up in front of the café, the door opened. The stranger I had seen the day before stepped out and came to a stop with his hands on his hips. Looking at Finn from the sidewalk, he said, "What is it?"

Finn drew himself up to his full height. "Is your name Paul Pimentel?"

The man glanced at me. "That's what I told your workman here."

"I heard you were looking for me."

"I didn't say that."

"I heard you came by my place and was askin' questions about me."

"If your name's Finn Cole, that's true."

"Well, I don't like people comin' by my place when I'm not there, and I don't like people askin' questions about me."

"Neither of those things is against the law."

Finn's face stiffened. "I don't know what your game is. You sound a little too smart to me. Why don't you step down here into the street and back up your smart words?"

"Take off your gunbelt, and I will."

By now, a few onlookers had gathered, and everyone could see that Pimentel was not wearing a gun.

Finn unbuckled his belt and handed it, along with the holster and six-gun, to me. As if on second thought, he took off his hat and gave it to me as well.

Pimentel stepped forward, took hold of a post that held up the awning, and turned his back to us as he swung down into the street. As he did so, he slipped his right hand into his pants pocket. When he drew it out, I saw him close his fist around a pocketknife with a short, thick, brown handle. I did not know how many others, if any, saw the movement.

When he stood around square in the street, he took off his hat with his left hand, and with a bit of a flourish, he sailed it onto the sidewalk. He put up his fists with his forearms curved and his elbows forward, as I had seen boxers do. He gave a mocking smile and said, "Come on."

Finn moved forward with what I imagined was his own sure method. He settled on his left foot and swung with his left fist, trying to knock down his opponent's guard. Then he stepped forward with his right foot and swung a right punch.

Pimentel stepped back, bounced on his feet, and came in with a straight-arm left jab that shook Finn's head. Then he came across with a hard right punch that caught Finn on the jaw and cheek and dropped him to the ground. As Pimentel stood back, he slipped his right hand into his pocket and brought it out empty. With his palm upward, he said, "Is that good enough for the moment?"

Finn raised himself to one elbow and rubbed the side of his face. "I guess so. But this isn't the last of it."

Pimentel shrugged. "Either of us could decide that."

I was cleaning the stall later that day when Evie came from the house. She was wearing a brown dress and hat, which helped give her eyes a light brown tone. She had a worried expression like the day before, and she was clutching one hand with the other. I waited as she drew within four feet of me and spoke in a low voice.

"You didn't tell Finn what I told you, did you? About my thinking there was something familiar about that stranger?"

I shook my head. "I didn't say anything about our conversation. He didn't ask me, and I didn't volunteer anything."

"He got it out of me that someone had come by, and so I had to tell him I talked to you. But I didn't tell him anything about that strange sense I had."

"Well, he's seen him for himself by now, anyway."

"That's what I heard. He's furious about it. He said the man caught him off guard and hit him with something. I'm sure he wants to get even."

I twisted my mouth and nodded my head. "Seemed that way to me."

Finn and Holbrook returned from their afternoon ride as the sun was going down. I was slicing potatoes, as it was my turn to cook, and I saw them through the open door.

Holbrook came into the bunkhouse in a huff. He said, "Let's not take too long with supper. Finn wants to go into town, and he wants both of us to go with him."

We hurried through the meal, cleaned up, and grabbed our hats. Finn was waiting for us with a horse already saddled for himself. Holbrook and I made short work of catching and saddling horses for ourselves. The night was dark, but the horses knew the trail, and we made it to town almost as soon as we did in the daylight.

Finn and Holbrook led the way to the Buckeye Saloon. We tied up at the rail and walked into the lamplight of the saloon. It was not a large establishment, maybe twenty-five feet wide and thirty-five feet deep. Men stood along the bar, and a few sat at tables.

Halfway down the bar, Paul Pimentel stood with his left

elbow on the bar and his right hand on his hip, in a posture that allowed him to watch the front door. As before, he was not wearing a gun.

Holbrook and Finn walked up to him, with me following. Pimentel's eyes roved over both of them.

"What do you need?" he said.

To my surprise, Holbrook answered. "You seemed pretty sure of yourself earlier in the day. How would you like to try your luck with me?"

Pimentel raised his eyebrows. "Take off your gunbelt, and I'll give you a gentleman's chance."

"Sure." Holbrook stepped back, and with a smirk on his face, he unbuckled the gunbelt and handed it to me.

The bartender came bustling from the far end of the bar. "See here," he said. "If you're going to fight, you need to take it outside."

Pimentel held up his left hand and said, "This won't take long." With a swirl of the hand, he took off his hat and set it on the bar. At the same time, he slipped his right hand into his trousers pocket and brought it out in a fist.

Men stepped back to give the two fighters room, and the men sitting at the tables scraped the chair legs as they stood up.

Pimentel raised his fists in front of him, tossed his head, and said, "Come on."

Holbrook, lighter on his feet than I expected, bounced in, tossed a punch that hit Pimentel's forearms, and bounced back. From out of nowhere, it seemed, he produced a shiny-bladed knife that he opened with a flick of the wrist and a click.

A gasp went around the small crowd.

Holbrook said, "You've got a knife in your hand. Use it."

Pimentel's face fell as a mutter went through the crowd.

Holbrook made a thrust forward, with his hand and elbow high. Pimentel jumped back, keeping an eye on the shiny blade.

Holbrook lunged again, taking a swipe that cut the sleeve on Pimentel's shirt as he raised his arm in defense.

No one made a move to interfere. Holbrook leapt forward again, this time with his arm low and the cutting edge of the blade up.

Pimentel, moving back and to the side, kept an eye on the knife. "So this is the way it is," he said. "Like before." His chest went up and down. "I know who you are."

Pimentel brought his hands together to open his knife, and Holbrook rushed him. Holbrook pushed with his left arm against Pimentel's raised forearms, and with his right hand lower, he drove the knife blade into Pimentel's midsection.

Pimentel hunched and stood back, dropping his unopened knife and pressing his hand against his stomach. Blood leaked between his fingers. His eyes widened, and his face went pale as he raised his head. He said, "You low-down sons of bitches. Takes two of you. Just like you did with Pete." His eyes rolled up, and he brought them back. He blinked. Tears started in his eyes. He pressed his upper teeth against his lower lip, and he seemed to be trying to pull together the strength to say something more, but he lost everything and slumped to the floor.

"You all saw it," said Holbrook. "The man had a knife, so I took it to him on his terms."

I had dug out a broken corral post and was tamping in a new one, sweating on a hot and hazy afternoon, when Evie came my way at a determined pace from the house. Finn and Holbrook had gone off on an afternoon ride, as they often did, and I imagined she had been waiting for them to leave.

She was wearing a light blue dress and a cloth hat, and her eyes had a bluish-grey cast to them. Her face was clouded, and her voice quavered as she said, "What happened? I know something bad happened, but Finn won't tell me."

I took in a full breath to steady my own nervousness. "There was a fight," I said. "Holbrook goaded the other man into it. The stranger had a way of wrapping his fist around a short, thick pocketknife, the way some men use a brass bar or a lead weight or something similar. That's how he knocked Finn down. But Ross was ready for him and shook out a knife with about a five-inch blade, what I've heard some people call a stiletto. He got the best of the stranger with it."

Evie seemed to sink as the breath went out of her. "I was afraid something like that would happen, that they would . . . take care of him. Did he say anything, this Paul Pimentel?"

"He did. Something strange to me, but I think it had meaning for Finn and Ross."

Evie's eyes were wide open. "What was it?"

I moistened my lips. I felt that I had to tell her. "He said he knew who Ross was, and it was like before. They were doing to him what they did to Pete."

Evie gasped. "He said that name?"

"Yes, he did. It was the last thing he said."

Tears were falling as Evie shook her head. "I knew it. I knew it. I knew there was something familiar about him."

I wanted her to tell me more, so I prompted her. "About Pimentel?"

"Yes, but I'm sure that wasn't his name. I think he was Pete's brother, come to get even."

All this time, I had been holding the shovel upside down, as I had been tamping the post with the tip of the handle. I turned the shovel right side up and rested the blade on the ground. I said, "Who was Pete?"

She had fear in her eyes as she looked at me straight and said, "You can't tell anybody I told you."

"I won't." At the same time, I was uneasy about what I might hear at this point.

She sniffed as she took in a deep breath. She swallowed and exhaled. "Pete was the one I was with before . . . before Finn. They all worked together—Pete, Finn, and Ross—in some kind of a gang, I think. I didn't ask questions. But they made money, in some way. Then one day they had a fight among them— about money, of course, or at least that was what I was told. They said it was a fair fight and Ross came out on top. Pete didn't. Finn said we had to get out of there. Things were too hot. So we came here, and he bought this place, and they've been carrying on like normal citizens ever since."

"And so you just . . . ended up with Finn?"

Evie's eyes did not meet mine. "I'm ashamed to say it, but yes. I felt I needed the protection, and he has a way of making a woman feel as if she's under his power."

I had heard women say things like that before, and I didn't think I could do anything about her situation. I said, "Who was Paul Pimentel, then?"

"Pete's brother, I'm sure. That's why I thought I recognized something about him. But the name wasn't Pimentel. It was Hester. And Pete didn't ever mention a brother named Paul. He only spoke of one named Jim."

"So this fellow, Paul or Jim, came to get even for what they did to his brother."

"I think so. I believe he was in prison for a while, so it might have taken him this long to finish his sentence and then find out where Finn was."

I was feeling a little steadier now. I was beginning to form an understanding of the whole situation, and I felt as if I was on the outside of it all. I said, "Not that it matters much now, but where did this earlier part take place?"

"In the mining country in Colorado. Up around Leadville."

I had a general idea of where that was. I said, "Well, the

ranch country in Wyoming is an unsuspecting place."

Her blue-grey eyes met me now. "You have to promise me you won't tell anyone I told you any of this."

"I already told you I wouldn't."

Her voice sounded calm as she said, "I'm done with him. I have to find a way to get away from him."

My pulse picked up. A few seconds earlier, I felt as if I was on the outside, and now I felt as if I was being pulled in. "Do you think you can?" I asked.

"I have to."

In that moment I did not see her as an outlaw's woman, though I did not know what one would be like. But I saw her as a desirable woman, and that did not do me any good. I knew I should be making a plan to get as far away as possible. But instead I said, "Do you think you can do it by yourself?"

Her eyes met mine again as she said, "If I need help, I'll tell you."

Finn showed up in a calm mood at the bunkhouse the next morning. Sometimes he smoked tailor-made cigarettes, and on this occasion, he drew a small case out of his vest pocket and took out a cigarette with neat, packed ends. He rapped it on his thumbnail, put it in his mouth, and lit it.

"Dan," he said, "I need you to go to the place up north for a couple of days. Get a precise count on the cows and calves in that pasture, and patch any weak spots in the fence. I think some of them have been gettin' out, and I don't know if any of them have strayed."

"I'll do it," I said. "How much grub should I take?"

"Figure enough for one night and two days. You can be back here for supper tomorrow night."

I counted the meals. "All right."

"And clean up the kitchen here before you go. Ross and I

have a long day ourselves."

"I will."

I finished my coffee and began picking up my own plate, the platter the bacon had been on, and the tin plate that had held the biscuits. I wondered if Finn and Holbrook were up to something. They had been keeping close company for the last few days and had been leaving me to work on my own. Now Finn was sending me several miles north, where he leased two sections of fenced pasture. I knew the place well enough, including the shanty we used as a line shack.

I had finished the cleanup and was putting a few personal items in my war bag when I heard a knock at the back door. I took soft steps across the room and cracked the door open.

Evie whispered, "Quick. I've only got a minute."

I opened the door and saw her pale, worried face. "What is it?" I asked.

She spoke in a rush. "Finn's in the outhouse, and Ross is getting their horses ready. I can't let them catch me here. But I had to tell you. We're on our own now."

"What do you mean?"

"I told him I was thinking of leaving, and he knocked all the resistance out of me. He has his ways. He told me I was never going to leave. Then he got it out of me that you told me what happened in town the night before last. I'm sorry I told him, but I couldn't help it. I was on my back, in bed. He had his full weight on me, and he had his hands on my throat." She was wringing her hands, and fear showed in her eyes. "I'm sorry. I have to go. But I had to tell you."

I studied her lost expression. I didn't know what to say or do. I was trying to take it all in.

Still in a whisper, she said, "I couldn't do anything else. I have to run now. I'm sorry. And Dan—"

"Yes?"

"If we both get out of this, I'd like to see you again."

She was gone on a fast run, a grey dress retreating in the clear light of morning.

I shook my head as I tried to catch up with what I had just heard. Finn was onto us, both of us. He knew why Evie wanted to leave, and he knew that I knew. I remembered what Evie had said the first day the stranger came by. She didn't expect anything good to come of this. I was beginning to agree.

My first impulse was to tie my bag on the back of the saddle and ride like hell as fast and as far as I could go. But a few things worked together to make me go through the motions of doing what the boss told me. First, I did not have my own horse, so if I went anywhere out of line, I could be accused of stealing another man's horse. Second, no matter where I went, I could count on Ross Holbrook tracking me down. He wouldn't take the trouble to brace me in front of other men. A bullet in the back would be fine with him. A queasy feeling ran between my shoulder blades.

Then there was Evie. I had the flaw of not being able to see where she was at fault. I found it plumb easy to see how Finn was crooked and corrupt, and I despised the idea that a man could take the woman of a man he had killed or had had killed. And Evie had gone with him. I couldn't get past that, but I couldn't focus on it strong enough to make me decide I should get out of this spot any way I could and run like hell. I wanted to get out, but I wanted to see if she would, too.

So I went on about packing my things, along with a bait of grub. I carried my bag and my bedroll out to the barn, where I left them in the hay while I picked out a horse.

I selected a dark horse that I often rode. He was brownish-black with a thick, black mane and tail, and he had black lower legs. Some people would call him a bay. I just called him a dark horse. I chose him because he could go all day and never get tired, and because he did not have any light markings that could be seen at night.

Finn and Holbrook were lolling around at the hitching rail in front of the house, smoking cigarettes. For as much as they had a long day ahead of them, they didn't seem to be in a hurry. I assumed they were waiting for me to leave first, and I would be a bigger fool than I already was if I doubled around and came back to talk to Evie. So I saddled the horse, tied on my gear, and waved to Finn and Holbrook as I set out on my way to the place up north.

I had the cattle counted by noon of the first day. The pasture consisted of only two sections, rolling country with no side canyons or hidey-holes. I came up with twenty-three cows and twenty-three calves, the same number we had put into the pasture some six weeks earlier, and the same number we had counted more than once in the meanwhile. I thought that Finn's concern about stock getting loose was a fish story, but orders were orders. With my gear stowed in the shack, I found the fence pliers, staples, and hammer, and I spent the afternoon riding fence and fixing weak spots.

I put the dark horse in the small corral as the sun slipped in the west. I had noticed earlier that there was a small stack of firewood inside, by the cast-iron stove. I split a few of the larger pieces with the loose-handled ax that stood in the corner by the stove wood, and I built a fire to fry the salt pork I had brought along. I left the door of the shack open, to let out the heat and to make it easier for me to keep a lookout.

I did not think that Holbrook would come for me in daylight. I more or less assumed he would come, just as I assumed that Finn would stay at home and keep an eye on Evie.

The sun went down, and a red-orange moon between a quarter and a half hung in the sky to the south. I plumped up my blankets to make my bedding look as if someone might be sleeping there, and I took my place behind the door.

I had not waited very long when I began to wonder whether I would have the calmness of mind and the steadiness of hand to fire a straight shot in the dark. I thought of an option. I crept across the room, found the ax in the faint light that came in the window, and tipped it up to let the head slide off. With the handle in my hands, I took a seat behind the door again.

I waited about two hours, and nobody came. I began to doubt my own judgment. Then I told myself that if I let my guard down, someone would come. For all I knew, a man like Holbrook might know when a victim was most likely to be in his deepest sleep, or in more general terms, he might know when all sleeping things were at their lowest ebb. That would be the time to be on the prowl.

My uneasiness began to eat on me. I wondered if anyone was going to do anything. I wondered if anyone was doing anything out of the ordinary back at the ranch.

My worry and my curiosity got the best of me. I saddled the dark horse and made ready to go take a look. I left my belongings and the grub in the line shack, but I took the ax handle.

The horse and I made good time in the thin moonlight, and I slid off to walk the last half-mile into the ranch. I took off my spurs, put them in the saddlebag, and left my hat on the saddle horn. Light was showing through the cracks in the barn, which did not surprise me. I tied the dark horse to a corral post in back, and holding the ax handle at my side, I made my way to the door. Light spilled out where the door was ajar, so I edged up to get a peek.

My stomach thumped at the sight of Finn Cole and Ross Holbrook, smoking cigarettes in the lamplight. They stood by the hind ends of three horses, one of which was saddled. Only Holbrook was wearing a hat, but both of them wore gunbelts.

Finn's voice carried. "We can get up there and back in a little more than two hours. Take care of numskull, leave her off, and go into town in the morning."

I wondered if I heard him right. What he said didn't make sense until I realized how many horses were tied up. I shifted to get a better look inside, and what I saw sent my blood to my feet.

Evie's body lay in a heap on the straw. She was wearing the same grey dress she was wearing when I saw her alive for the last time.

I did not know whether Finn had planned to do her in or if he had done so in the height of an argument, but it was evident what he and Holbrook were planning to do from this point on. They were going to make it look as if Evie had gone to the line shack to see me, I had done violence to her, and they had caught me red-handed.

Finn's voice rose again. "I need to go to the house. Go ahead and saddle these other two, and I'll be back in a few minutes."

Holbrook nodded, then palmed his face as he took a drag off of his cigarette. He did not seem bothered by the work at hand.

I sank back into the shadows as Finn walked out and left the door half-open. His spurs clinked as he continued on his way to the house.

I crept to the door and took another look. Holbrook had his back to me as he laid the blanket on the back of a sorrel horse and swung the saddle up and onto the blanket. He bent down, reached under, and pulled the cinch to him. When he straightened up again, he had the cigarette sticking out of the side of his mouth as he ran the latigo through the cinch ring and then the D ring on the saddle.

I told myself it was now or never. I took the quietest steps I could, came up behind him, and raised the ax handle to shoulder level with both hands. The sorrel horse nickered, Ross

Holbrook turned around, and the last thing he saw was the ax handle coming full force at the side of his head.

His hat fell away, and he went down like a sack of potatoes. I took in a quick, deep breath. Finn would be back any time, and I did not know if I would be lucky enough to do the same thing twice.

I heard footsteps and the light jingle of spurs. I did not have time to move to the side of the door, and because it opened outward, I would not have had a good hiding place anyway. I moved to the third horse and stood crouched on the other side of its hip.

Finn came into the lamplight at a jaunty pace, wearing a hat and carrying something I did not recognize at first. He stopped short, transferred the object to his left hand, and laid his right hand on his gun. I saw then that the object he carried was a small set of saddlebags, the kind that a rider drapes over the swells in front.

"Ross," he said. "Is there something wrong with you?" He squinted his eyes, looked to both sides, and moved forward. He started to kneel, then stood up and looked around again.

I could tell he had not placed me yet. With my gun drawn, I stepped to the hind end of the horse, stood sideways to give him less of a target, and aimed.

He drew his gun quicker than I would have imagined, but he did not make a good enough shot. I felt my left arm jerk backward with the impact of a bullet as my right forefinger pulled the trigger.

Finn Cole spilled over backwards and to the left, dropping his pistol and falling on the little set of saddlebags. As he went down, I saw a dark spot staining his vest.

I walked over to the place where Evie's body lay slumped in the straw. My voice did not sound strange to me as I said, "I'm sorry you didn't get more of a chance, Evie."

Though I had plenty of contempt for Finn and Holbrook, I had nothing more for a speech. My left arm was stinging and throbbing, so I rolled up my sleeve. A gouge had been taken out of the flesh on my lower arm, but as far as I could tell, no bone was broken, and no blood vessel was cut. The wound was bleeding, but the blood was not welling out.

Everything was quiet and still as I tore strips from my sleeve and used my teeth to tighten a bandage around my wound. The horses had jumped and grunted and crowded when the shots were fired, but they were quieted down now.

I had a dizzy sensation, a strange sense that I had lived through some of this before or that it had to happen as it did. I shook my head to be sure I was not dreaming. There was no changing what had taken place.

I walked out of the barn and into the faint moonlight. My mouth was dry, but my mind was clearing. My thoughts ranged from small to large. I realized there were two things I would never know—what Finn had in the little saddlebags, and whether I could have killed a man and ended up with his woman.

I shook my head again, slower this time. I wasn't even sure I could kill a man until I saw what happened to Evie. Then there was no question.

I stood near the barn for a moment, breathing the night air and focusing on what I had to do next. Taking the horse of a man who had planned to kill me did not bother me a bit. I made my way out back, pulled myself into the saddle with one hand, and rode the dark horse away, into the night.

★ ★ ★ ★ ★

DARKNESS IN BURNETT

★ ★ ★ ★ ★

Dearing let the grey horse pick its way down the hill through the sagebrush, where clumps of soapweed held out their daggerlike blades. The rangeland was awakening from winter in its slow way, as if from a warming in the earth's center, but the cloud cover that spread in all directions subdued the sunlight. Light patches of new grass were beginning to show, and the first carpet flowers appeared with thin white petals and narrow, pale-green leaves.

Down through the swale and up the other side, the rustle of saddle leather mixed with the thud of hooves on damp earth and the heaving breath of the horse.

On a south-facing crest that held another scattering of the thin, white ground lilies, Dearing brought the horse to a rest. Half a mile away, a horse and rider moved toward him. Dearing took in the pair at a glance, recognizing Trent Malone and the dark horse he had saddled that morning.

The song of a meadowlark carried over the sagebrush and grass, then died in the air.

As Dearing waited, Malone's features came into view—his wavy brown hair, blue eyes, and rosy cheeks. In the dent of the peaked crown of his hat, he wore a blue hatpin that matched the color of his neckerchief.

Malone drew his horse to a stop and brought out the makings. As he began to roll a cigarette, he asked the usual question. "See anything?"

"Nothing to speak of. Just cows and calves. Didn't see a snake. I don't know if they're out yet."

Malone pushed out his lower lip and shook his head. "Don't think so." He kept his eyes on his cigarette until he raised it to lick the seam. He paused and said, "Here's Wilmer."

Dearing followed Malone's glance. A rider with his hat brim turned up in front came boiling across the country. He had his elbows out, and the tails of his wheat-colored canvas coat flapped in the dull daylight.

Wilmer's horse bunched up as it came to a stop. The rider tipped forward and settled back. " 'Bout got a problem."

Malone had lit his cigarette and had it tucked in the web of his first two fingers. He laid his hand across the lower part of his face as he took a drag. He blew away the smoke and said, "What do you mean?"

Wilmer had his eyes open wide. "Found a girl dead."

"Who did?"

"Her family. Nesters called Redmond. Over by Chalk Butte."

"I know where they live." Malone rubbed his nose. "When did it happen?"

"I guess they found her yesterday. So it happened the night before."

"Was she sick?"

Wilmer's eyes widened again. "No. She went out the window."

Malone frowned. "What do you mean?"

"She snuck out at night, and somebody got her."

"Oh, hell."

"It's what I heard."

"Just wanderin' on the prairie at night?"

Wilmer pulled in a breath, and his eyes half-closed. "They think she met someone."

"Oh, well, that's different."

"Sure is." Wilmer turned to Dearing. "You fellows are headed back, I suppose."

Dearing nodded. "We just met up. We might as well ride in together. Unless you're supposed to meet Endicott."

"I can ride in with you."

Malone took a long drag on his cigarette, flicked the ash, and held the stub sideways. "Did you know this girl?"

Wilmer sniffed as he shook his head. "Just know of her."

Malone took one last pull on the cigarette and pinched it out. "Might as well get movin'."

The three riders set out, with a jingle of bits and spurs. Dearing said, "What was the girl's name?"

"Redmond," said Wilmer. "I don't know her first name."

Malone remained silent.

Dearing did not form much of a picture. It all seemed rather distant, just a girl with a last name, who sneaked out at night and met the wrong person.

Warmth poured out of the open door of the cast-iron stove. Dearing, Wilmer, and Endicott sat in the glow, and a few minutes later, Vince, the cook, joined them to make a semicircle. With supper finished, the dishes put away, and Malone having gone to the ranch house to talk to the boss, the other four men in the bunkhouse took up the topic of the day.

Wilmer seemed to enjoy being the bearer of the news, as if he was the proprietor of the story. "So this nester family, name of Redmond, went lookin' for their daughter when she turned up missing in the morning. They found her dead on the ground about a hundred yards from the house. They think she'd been goin' out the window for a while. But it was one time too many. She had bruise marks on her throat. They think she was choked."

"Choked," said Endicott. He stretched out his stovepipe boots and took the toothpick from the corner of his mouth.

Vince frowned. "When did it happen?"

105

"They found her yesterday, so it would have been night before last. Word got around after they took her to town."

Dearing kept his thoughts to himself, but he recalled the image of seeing Malone's empty bunk in the middle of the night.

Endicott sat up and cleared his throat. "I don't like to say anything, but I believe it was two nights ago that Trent slipped out for a while. I don't know for how long. I woke up around midnight and saw he was gone, and when I woke up again in the mornin', he was there. Wasn't the first time, and like I say, I don't like to say anything. What a man does is his business."

Wilmer put on a thoughtful look. "It would be a long ride. You don't even know that he went somewhere. Did anyone hear hoofbeats?"

Dearing shook his head.

Vince scratched at his thinning white hair. "I don't hear much from where I sleep. That's why I have my bed there."

Dearing nodded. The cook had a small nook, the size of a pantry, off the side of the kitchen, where he went to bed early and got up early.

Endicott said, "I couldn't say that I heard anything. But sometimes you wake up, and you don't remember hearing anything, but maybe you did."

"Puh," said Wilmer. "I don't think he would do something like that. I know Trent, and I just don't think he would do it." He turned to Dearing. "What do you think, Jim? You ride with him."

Dearing shrugged. "I don't know. You can ride with someone and talk about cows and horses and even girls, but that doesn't mean you know anything." He shook his head. "I don't like talkin' about him when he just stepped out for a while."

Endicott chewed on his toothpick. "But if someone in our midst was doing something, or had done something, and if one of us knew something, we shouldn't pretend that nothing happened."

"Oh, no. If I knew something, it would be different."

Wilmer took in a full breath. "Well, I know Trent. And I don't think he would do something like that. What do you think, Vince?"

The cook poked his finger into the bowl of his pipe and moved his lips without speaking.

"Go ahead," said Wilmer.

Vince put the pipestem in his mouth and took it out. "I don't want to judge anyone. But I've heard a few people in my time say what you just did. 'I know so-and-so, and I know he wouldn't do that.' Turns out the fella goes out at night and burns down houses, or he plays with little kids in an indecent way, or—"

"I didn't say I knew he wouldn't. I said I didn't think he would."

Vince shrugged. "Good enough. Still, you say you know him. My point is, you never know someone for sure, not all the way. People are capable of too much. If someone does something deep and dark and wrong, he'll do anything he can to keep others from knowing it."

Wilmer raised his eyebrows and gave a small laugh. "I'd almost think you'd done somethin' yourself."

"Don't worry about me. I'm just makin' the simple point that you never know someone for sure. There are too many surprises that tell otherwise."

The aroma of fried bacon hung in the air as Dearing poured himself a cup of coffee and handed the pot to Wilmer. Rattling came from the end of the table, where Vince was sliding the breakfast plates into the dishpan. When the noise died down, Malone spoke.

"I understand some of you might have a doubt about where I've gone to on a night."

Dearing glanced at Wilmer, who twisted his mouth and said nothing.

Malone had rolled and lit a cigarette, and he held it out and away from him with the tips of two fingers. "I don't blame anyone for talking. I'd do the same thing if I thought something shady, or should I say, against the law, had gone on. But nothing did. And I know you all know that what a man does on his own is his business and not someone else's. All the same, I don't mind saying something that as a general rule I'd keep to myself. Just to be clear." He took a drag on his cigarette. "If I happened to be gone for a while in the night, it wasn't to go see some nester girl."

With all eyes on Malone, Dearing allowed himself to observe him. The man had a self-assurance that Dearing had known earlier, in fellows back home. Dearing had sensed that it came from having a good build, good looks, and some success with women. He had wondered why girls, or women, were willing to please some men, even to the point, as he saw it, of throwing themselves away and marrying men who then lorded it over them. He had seen it in his own sister, before she had the good fortune of being jilted. That fellow had had a pretty aspect about him like Malone did, with his sparkling eyes and rosy cheeks.

Malone tapped his ash in a sardine can. "I didn't want to have to say this much, but I will, just to be on the level with you fellas. I did go out at night, and on more than one occasion, but I can't say where because I have to protect the reputation of a woman. I'd rather be accused of a crime I didn't commit than betray the confidence of a lady."

Dearing felt himself settle in his seat as his breath went out. It was a strange kind of relief, like being subdued more than convinced, and he sensed it in the other two punchers.

Wilmer said, "Well, no one asked you to account for yourself. I think you said more than you had to, but I'm willing to leave it at that."

Malone raised his chin. "So am I." He turned to the cook, who had resumed rattling the plates and silverware in the dishpan. "What do you think, Vince?"

Silence hung in the air. By tradition, the cook had authority over the kitchen, the bunkhouse, and the chuck wagon. Dearing imagined that Malone had heard some of what Vince had said the night before and wanted to challenge him in front of the other men.

Vince looked up, and his grey eyes were calm. "I don't know. I wasn't there."

A faint change of expression stole over Malone's face. Dearing saw it as resentment. In that moment, he thought, *Someone was there. Someone knows.*

Dearing rode into the ranch yard by himself as the evening shadows lengthened. He and Malone had agreed to come in each on his own and be able to check on cattle outside of the regular pattern that the men rode. Dearing did not have a sense of whether Malone wanted to avoid him, but he thought it was just as well. All day long, as he looked in draws and box canyons, thoughts of the Redmond girl came back to him. He did not have a mental picture of her, just a faceless impression of a girl who went out into the night and met her end. Dearing told himself it was not his fault, but he was nagged all the same by an awareness that such a thing could happen in the simple world where he had come to make a living. It was not his fault, but he would be going along with it unless he did what he was making his mind up to do.

He put his horse away and knocked on the ranch house door.

Footsteps sounded, and the door opened to show the boss, Rich Farrow. He was a tall man, with stooped shoulders and a forward-leaning bald head. He was wearing glasses and held a newspaper by his side. His left hand rested on the doorknob.

"What is it?"

Dearing fumbled his words, though he had rehearsed them. "I'd like to ask for my pay, sir."

Farrow drew his bushy brows together. "Is there something wrong?"

"Nothing to speak of. I just feel that I need to move on."

"We're a long ways from a train whistle. Is someone on your heels?"

"Oh, no, sir. Not at all. It just seems like it's time for me to go."

The boss looked him up and down. "I suppose. How much of a hurry are you in? I can figure your pay and have it ready in the morning."

"That would be all right. I'd just as soon not pass any remarks to the others this evening, though."

The boss nodded as if he was taking something in. "I don't plan to talk to anyone else tonight anyway. But tell me this. Did you know that girl who died?"

"No, sir. I wouldn't know her if I saw her. I don't even know her first name."

"It's just as well. Malone told me about it, and it doesn't sound good." The boss moved the door an inch. "I'll see you in the morning, then."

"Thank you. Good night."

Dearing rode into Burnett at midmorning. The main street ran north and south, so the west side lay in full sunlight. He stopped his horse at the hitching rail in front of the post office and barbershop, swung his leg high over his bedroll and war bag,

110

and settled to the ground. As he tied the reins, he nodded to a man sitting on the bench in front of the barbershop. Dearing walked into the post office, arranged to have his mail held until further notice, and stepped out into the warming sunlight.

The man on the bench, an older fellow with a stubbled beard and a slouch hat, raised his hand in a wave. Dearing had placed him as the man who worked the night shift at the livery stable, and now the name came to him. Wim O'Connor.

Dearing paused and said, "Good morning."

"And the same to you. What's in the wind?"

"Not much. I'm leaving town, for a while at least, and I asked 'em to hold any mail that might come."

The old man squinted. "If I had any mail, I'd look at the return address, to make sure it wasn't a mistake."

"Same with me."

The stableman creased his face again. "This is the time of year fellas like you come here, to work the season. Did you find a better job?"

"No, I just decided to leave."

"Huh. Has anything got you down?"

"No, I'm just leaving."

"I don't mean to ask too many questions." The old man gave what Dearing thought was a knowing look and said, "I don't blame you. Sometimes things aren't right for a fella where he is."

Dearing made a small nod, although he wasn't sure if he was agreeing with an idea. He felt as if something hung in the air, but he didn't know if he imagined it. He knew that the back part of the barbershop was a kind of undertaker's parlor, where bodies were prepared for burial. He wondered if the girl had been brought into that room, or was even there at the moment—and if so, whether the old man was sitting in the sunlight with that knowledge. Dearing's senses swam for a second, and

111

he came back to himself. He could not have asked the question, and now the instant had passed.

"I guess I'll be going," he said. "Maybe I'll see you if I come back through."

"Might as well. I'm always here."

Dearing followed the trail north, riding through the same kind of rangeland he had been working. With the reappearance of some details, such as sagebrush, soapweed, and thin white carpet flowers, he had a returning awareness of the girl for whom he had nothing more than a last name. He pushed away at the feeling of guilt that crowded on him, but he could not escape the sense that he was turning his back on her.

New impressions came to him as he rode into the town of Devereux at the close of day. People counted it a full day's ride from Burnett, so he had made good time. The mild weather had helped, and the clear sky at sundown had a relaxing effect, as if this new locale did not hold complications.

He found a place where lantern light fell on the sidewalk and voices carried on the air. A sign that hung from the awning identified the saloon as The Trace. Dearing dismounted, tied up, and went in.

A row of three overhead lamps made the interior seem bright in comparison with the dusk outside. Dearing walked to the bar that ran along the left side. The bartender, catching him in the mirror, turned around to reveal a square-built man with a high forehead, dark eyes, and a mustache that looked like the bristle end of a black paintbrush. He put both hands on the bar and smiled with his mouth closed.

"What'll it be, pal?"

"A glass of beer." Dearing laid a two-bit piece on the bar.

"Comin' up." The bartender turned in a rigid motion and began to draw the beer.

A man standing a few feet down the bar said, "I'll take one while you're at it, Seymour."

The bartender took up a second glass and watched his patrons in the mirror. He swiveled back with a glass in each hand and set them in front of Dearing and the other man. "Here you are."

Dearing sipped his beer and took a glance at the customer on his right. The man was shorter than average with a light-colored, high-crowned hat and a long, mushroom-colored canvas duster. He thrust out his lower jaw, moved his head forward, and settled back.

The bartender had taken Dearing's quarter and now laid down a dime in change. "Did you come up the trail today?"

"Yes, I did."

The other man moved his head a quarter of a turn. "From Burnett?"

"Yes, I left there this morning."

"I heard they just had a death down that way."

"I heard that, too."

The man moved his jaw like before. "Did the water get hot for you?"

Dearing frowned. "For me? No, not at all."

"Just wonderin'. Heard it was a girl got killed. Wasn't that it, Seymour?"

"It's what I heard."

The short man gave Dearing a wide eye. "And you don't know anything about it."

Dearing felt his anger rise, and he knew he had to keep it down. "I didn't have a thing to do with it, if that's what you mean. And as far as that goes, there's a much more likely suspect than I am." As soon as he spoke, he thought he might have said too much.

The other man shrugged. "Just curious." He tipped up his

glass and drank about half the contents. He lowered it, belched, and drank the rest. He set the glass down, then lifted his hat and rubbed the top of his head. He had short-cropped hair like a jail dock, with a receding hairline, although he didn't look much older than thirty. After settling his hat in place, he pushed away from the bar. "All for me. For now."

"Put this on your tab?"

"Sure." The man squared his shoulders, and with his fists half-closed, he strolled past Dearing toward the door.

Dearing watched in the mirror until he was sure the man was gone. "Prominent citizen?"

The bartender wiped the bar where the glass had been. "Name's Dawson Dowd. Not all that bad, I don't think. But he's been in a bad mood since he lost his job."

"Oh."

"He was workin' for a woman out by the Franklin Buttes. Widow by the name of Shipley. She let him go about a week ago."

"Well, that's not a good thing to happen to anyone."

"Nah, it isn't. I'd like to see him get another job. Meanwhile, I hope he doesn't run up too much of a tab. You know, sometimes when they do that, they leave town."

"Uh-huh." For as much as Dearing had seen of Dowd, he didn't care if the man left town. What interested him more was the prospect of finding work with the widow. He didn't think he would have to ask the bartender in order to learn where the Franklin Buttes were located.

Dearing found the Shipley ranch in a country of short grass and dark buttes—dark, he supposed, because of the damp air and grey cloud cover. The bare hills did not yet show any green, and he figured that the difference in climate came from being a ways farther north and a little higher in elevation.

As he approached the house, he was struck by the absence of sounds. In a normal ranch yard, he could expect to hear the neighing of horses, the lowing of cattle, or the barking of dogs. In hardscrabble country like this, he would not have been surprised to hear faint bells and the cry of sheep. But he heard nothing, and he saw no movement—not even a wisp of smoke from the stovepipe.

The house itself was a modest structure, maybe twenty-four feet square, with a pyramid roof. Most of the white paint had flaked off of the clapboard exterior, and the wooden shingles had turned grey with the weather. Behind the house, as Dearing rode into the yard, a long, low shed came into view. He imagined that it served as a barn or stable.

A door scuffed open, and a chicken squawked. A person stepped outside and stopped short. A set of denim overalls and a denim work coat did not show much of a shape, but a mass of hair, the color of old straw and not very well pinned up, gave the appearance of a woman.

Dearing swung down from the saddle and took off his hat. "Good morning," he said. "Is this the Shipley place?"

"It is."

He was distracted for a moment by the sight of an egg in her hand. He brought his attention back to her face. She had pale blue eyes and a weathered complexion, with the accumulation of flesh that came with early middle age. Dearing put on a smile and said, "Hoping not to be too forward, but I was given to understand that there might be work out this way."

The woman gave a light laugh. "Not many secrets in this country. I had a hired man and had to let him go. I don't know how soon I'll need another one."

"Oh."

"What do you know how to do? Count cows?"

"That, and a few other things. Rope and drag and brand.

Mark and cut. The season for that work is comin' up, of course."

"If I had cows."

He waited for her to say more.

"Up until last fall I had sheep. I'm on my own out here, you know. My husband ran sheep, and he would spend half the year out on the range with them. But it wasn't something I could do, and it was hard to find help I could rely on. There was always lambin' in bad weather, and a crew of sheepshearers at this time of year. I tell you, I was tired of it, and this last hired man I had, he talked me into selling the whole herd. Not that it took much. And he said he'd heard on many accounts, not least the almanac, that we were in for a bad winter. So I sold 'em all."

"I can understand why you might not need a hired man, then."

"Oh, I've got to do something with this place. I'm thinking of buying cattle, but I've got to be careful about how I go about it."

"Sure."

"And I need to get set up, which means to rebuild some corrals."

"I think I could handle that."

"Most cowpunchers think they know how to swing a hammer. But there's postholes to dig. There's also sheep manure to clean out when the weather is dry enough."

"I'm not afraid of working with a shovel."

"The last fellow seemed to be. But I'll tell you right out, that wasn't the only reason I had to get rid of him."

"Oh?"

"He was ambitious. I was convinced that he wanted to make the Shipley place into the Dowd place. That was his name, Dowd."

"I think I might have heard that."

"I doubt that he gave you much of a recommendation if you

met him. But I won't ask."

"I did happen to meet him, but our conversation was short, and he didn't mention this place or anyone here."

"Hah. Well, I guess I'll give you a try." She pointed with her thumb over her shoulder. "The hired man sleeps out here. Meals are in the kitchen. You'll hear the bell." She gave a curt nod and carried the egg to the house.

Snow was falling in heavy, wet flakes as Dearing trudged to the kitchen door. After a week of digging out rotten corral posts and salvaging planks, he had hoped things would dry out. But this late spring storm was bringing more moisture.

He shook off his hat and coat inside the door and turned a chair toward the stove. "Wet snow," he said.

"Yeah. I sure don't miss having lambs at a time like this. I don't know how many times we had 'em in the house, wet and sickly. But that was what made our livin'."

The aroma of fried meat wafted on the air, with an undercurrent of biscuits baking in the oven. Dearing imagined they were going to have salt pork for supper again. He didn't mind eating the same thing from one day to the next, and although the widow's biscuits were not light and fluffy, they were not heavy or burned, either.

"I'm going to make gravy," she said. "But I've got to take the meat out of the pan, so you might as well get started on it. The biscuits'll be out in a few minutes."

Dearing moved his chair to the table and raised his eyebrows as the sizzling meat slid onto his plate. He had learned from the beginning that the widow did not stand on ceremony but rather expected him to eat the grub as it came off the stove or out of the oven.

Sometimes the kitchen grew stuffy with the heat, but today the glow of the stove was just right as the snow swirled outside.

Dearing put away the fried meat, then the biscuits with gravy. The widow took a seat and ate her serving. Dearing thought the meal was done, but the widow surprised him with a pan of bread pudding with raisins and dried apples cooked in.

"Something to go with the coffee," she said.

In no hurry to go out into the storm, Dearing lingered over a second cup of coffee as the widow washed and rinsed the dishes. She asked him to pitch the dishwater, and when he returned from that task, she was seated again at the table. She had taken off her apron and had poured herself a cup of coffee.

"Cold and wet out there?" she asked.

"Yes, it is."

"Let's hope it's the last storm of the season, but you never know."

Dearing took his seat. Sometimes he felt like a child in the presence of this woman who was at least ten years older than he was, but she seemed sociable at the moment.

"So you met Mr. Dawson Dowd," she began.

"I did. But like I said before, we didn't converse for very long."

"What did he talk about, if you don't mind my asking?"

"Let me remember. Ah, yes. He and the bartender asked where I came from, and when I told them I had come up from Burnett, this fellow Dowd mentioned that a girl had died there."

"I heard about that, too."

"And he implied that I might have had something to do with it, and that was why I left."

"Oh, that's just like him. I don't imagine you did, or you wouldn't be telling me."

"Of course I didn't. The good part was that he didn't stay around for long."

"He stayed long enough here. Mooched for the whole winter.

I had to keep him at arm's length. You know, he wasn't very subtle."

Dearing wondered if she wanted to assure him that she hadn't had anything to do with Dowd. He shrugged and said, "I don't care much about him, one way or the other."

"That's just as well." She rose from her chair, walked a few steps to a cupboard, and reached down to open the door. She took out a bottle of whiskey and set it on the table.

"I would never have done this with him around. But I think I can trust you. A little nip to keep the storm at a distance."

Dearing awoke with a throbbing headache, a dry throat, and a feeling of dread in his stomach. Someone was snoring next to him in bed, and he realized it was the widow. He turned and saw that she had her throat wrapped in a towel. It looked damp, and he caught a strong odor suggestive of mint oil.

He shifted to turn his back on her, and his first thought was to put on his clothes and get away from there. He squeezed his eyes shut and opened them. Disconnected memories came back from the night before, laughing and clinking glasses with the widow in the lamplight in the kitchen, then the clumsy business of tumbling and mingling beneath the blankets.

As he sat up on the edge of the bed, she spoke.

"I suppose you want to leave, but you don't have to. This is just something we did. Don't worry about it. No one's going to hold anyone to anything. We can go back to where we were before. Stick to business. This doesn't change anything."

The sun at midday warmed the main street of town as Dearing tied the provisions onto the back of the saddle. He had everything on the list that Leah had given him, and he was trying to decide on an item she had not mentioned. At last he gave in to the side he thought he was leaning toward all along. Leaving the horse tied at the hitch rack, he directed his steps to The Trace.

The front door of the saloon was open, letting in the daylight. Except for the time of day, things had not changed in a week and a half. Seymour's blocky form took up space behind the bar, while Dawson Dowd leaned on the bar with his hat cocked and his duster hanging to his knees.

Seymour moved his brushlike mustache up and down and said, "What'll it be?"

Dearing tried not to let Dowd's presence affect him. "I'd like a quart of whiskey to take with me."

"I'll wrap one up." Seymour spread a wrinkled sheet of brown paper on the bar top, laid a whiskey bottle on its side, folded the paper and rolled the bottle, and twisted the package at the top as he set it upright. "There you go. Just a dollar and a quarter."

Dearing picked out the right coins and set them next to the package.

"Thanks. Workin' for the widow, are you?"

"Yes, I am."

"Thought I heard that."

Dowd's voice came up with a heavy tone of resentment. "When I worked there, she didn't let the hired hand have liquor on the place."

Dearing looked his way. "This is for someone else."

"I bet."

Dearing nodded to the bartender. "Thanks." He tucked the bottle in his arm and walked out into the sunlight.

Leah made a slight frown when Dearing handed her the bottle wrapped in brown paper. "I didn't expect you to do this."

"Seein' as how I helped you demolish the last one, I didn't think you'd mind."

"Oh, no. It's good to have on hand, this far from town." She opened the cupboard and stored the bottle in the shadows. "It'll keep."

Dearing draped his damp coat on the back of a chair and set it near the cookstove. Green grass was beginning to show in the pastures, but grey clouds had rolled in. The heat of the stove felt good on his open hands, and within a couple of minutes, tiny wisps of steam rose from the fabric of his coat.

Leah turned the pieces of beef that were frying in the skillet. "A few more minutes. You know, when I was a girl growing up on the farm, about once a month we'd have chicken on Sunday. But I've got so precious few here that I wouldn't think of cooking one."

"That's just the way things are."

"Oh, yeah. Nothing to be sorry for. Learn to do with what you've got."

That night he rolled in her bed again, not drunk this time, but relaxed with a few nips each. They played themselves out and went to sleep, but in the middle of the night he found himself with her again. In the first light of morning, he moved toward her one more time, and she responded as before.

At breakfast he tried to act as if nothing had happened, but he knew he made a poor job of it. At last he made himself speak.

"I don't know if I said anything I shouldn't have."

"No, you didn't. If you said anything at all, it was what people say in the night. It's like I said before. This is just for now. It's not going to last forever. We're both getting by, and it's all right for as long as it lasts. I know that sooner or later you'll move on, and I'm no fool. Not in some ways, at least. I know you'll want to meet someone who can give you a baby."

"I don't think about things like that."

"Not yet. But you will. Or at least I expect you will."

A succession of sunny days followed. The forces of life on the rangeland teemed in the air. More than once after noon dinner, lulled by good food and taken by desire, he buried his face in her bosom in the kitchen, and they waltzed to her bedroom. He lost count of how many times, and he did not think he had to keep track.

Soon it would be summer. Even now, Dearing had the illusion that the days would never change. At the same time, a voice from within reminded him that time moved on every day. Dark clouds would form in midsummer, and hail would come pelting. Frost would fall in October, or in late September in this country. Winter would come again and leave frozen carcasses in snowbanks.

Dearing shook his head and focused on the moment. He had planks to trim. Far away, his pals were currying their horses for spring roundup, if they hadn't already gone out. Spurs were jingling and music was playing in saloons and dance halls from Bozeman to Cheyenne.

Bozeman. That was where the musicians said they came from. He remembered them now, a man and a woman in a saloon in Lusk. The man was dressed in a brown coat and hat, and the woman wore yellow and black. She had blond hair like Leah's and might have been about the same age. The man played a mandolin, and the woman played a fiddle. They took turns singing songs, mostly sad ones. They sang one together, and two verses of it came back to Dearing now. He could hear the voices. The man sang,

> Meet me tonight in the moonlight,
> Leave your little sister at home.

Meet me in back of the churchyard,
Don't leave me to wait all alone.

Then came the woman's voice, wistful:

I'll meet you tonight at the churchyard,
When the moon's hanging bright overhead.
I won't tell my sister about us,
Though she sleeps next to me in our bed.

Dearing continued to saw on the weathered lumber. Other tunes came to him, including songs he sang out loud, but the song of the girl at the churchyard kept returning. He had heard people say that a strong tune worked that way. A person had to think of a stronger one to drive it out of his mind. He tried for the rest of the afternoon, and at some point, the music went away.

Dearing opened his eyes to the hazy light around him. He did not know if it was morning or evening. He knew where he was, though.

Leah's voice was soft but clear. "I'd better get supper started. Go ahead and rest for a while."

Dearing lay on his back and gathered his thoughts. He recalled a figure that had appeared to him just before he woke up. A man with a creased and stubbled face sat in the sunlight with a slouch hat shading his eyes. As Dearing stared at the ceiling in the fading light, he recalled his impression that the Redmond girl might have lain in the back room of the barbershop and that the man from the livery stable might know something. And even if he didn't, there was something to be known.

Dearing felt wide-awake now, as if a glow had caught on inside him. He was aware of things far away. Something wrong had happened. Somebody out there knew something, and even if one or more people tried to keep it hidden, the deed itself existed, under God's eye or whatever form of truth existed. If a person knew of the wrong and let it go unopposed, he was contributing to it. Dearing could not go back on that awareness, not now. It had come to light.

Leah smiled as he took his place at the table. "Are you all right?"

"Oh, yeah."

"You look as if something is troubling you."

"It's a small thing, and it's not about anything here."

She rapped the spoon on the edge of the pot where she was heating stew. "Well, that's all right."

He stared at her backside. He had not thought about how long he would stay here, taking life as it came. But now that he knew he had to leave, he saw that there was no delaying it.

"It's about something that happened in the last place where I was."

"Burnett."

"Yes. Or near there. I mentioned one time that a girl had been killed in that vicinity."

"I remember. I said I had heard about it."

Dearing hesitated, trying to find the right words. "Well, it has bothered me, and now it seems as if it has caught up with me. Not that I knew anything that nobody else did. But I just can't sit here knowing that somebody might be able to do something. I don't know what, but I feel that I need to go back now. Does that sound strange?"

"No. It sounds as if your conscience is gnawing on you, and not in a bad way."

"And you wouldn't take it wrong if I said I had to leave?"

She gave her light laugh. "Take it wrong. What have I said all along?"

He knew then that she was as good as her word and that his last night at the Shipley ranch would be all right.

Dearing followed the main trail and stopped in town to water his horse—and, as he admitted to himself, to see if there was any news of interest. When he saw Seymour sweeping debris out the front doorway of The Trace, he led his horse that way.

The bartender paused and let his eyes drift over the traveler and his horse. "Looks like you're packed up and ready to go somewhere."

"That's the case. It's time for me to move on."

"Things didn't last very long at the widow's. Seems to happen."

"Oh, there's nothing wrong with her. I don't know what Dowd might have said about her, but she's all right."

"Doesn't matter. He's gone, too. Off to mooch somewhere else, I expect."

"Sorry to hear that—or at least that he left you a bill, if he did."

"It's my fault. I should have known better. But they get you in for a dime, and the next thing you know, you're in for a dollar." Seymour cast a glance over the horse again. "Well, I wish you safe travels."

"Thanks. All the same to you."

Halfway to Burnett, Dearing veered east toward Chalk Butte. He knew that a tract of land out that way had been settled by homesteaders, and as he recalled, Wilmer had said the Redmond family lived there. With the afternoon sun at his back, he found the area that was divided up into half- and quarter-sections. Homesteader shacks stuck up here and there, and gaunt cattle stared at him from behind three strands of barbed wire. The grass was sparse where it grew. In some parcels, the ground had been plowed up and was struggling to put forth wheat, barley, and hay. To Dearing, it seemed like a place where poor people were trying to make a living on poor land.

He found a lane where a post had four boards nailed to it with a name on each. One of the names was Redmond. He turned down the lane, which appeared to be a section line, and he came upon a boy about ten years old who was tending to a nanny goat on a tether. The goat was eating grass and weeds between the road and the fence. Dearing asked the boy about who lived in the four quarter-sections, and the boy called them out as he pointed. Dearing thanked the boy and rode on.

The Redmonds had the second place on the left. As Dearing approached it, he noted a house about twenty feet by twenty-four, a stable about twelve by sixteen, and a haystack. Dearing did not have a plan for what he would say. He hoped he would think of something when he got there.

As he rode into the yard, he heard the lowing of cattle and the bawling of calves. A man appeared at the corner of a corral behind the stable. He leaned a pitchfork against the top rail and walked forward.

Dearing dismounted and stood by his horse.

The man had a hard, distrustful expression on his face. "What do you need?"

"Don't mean to bother you, but I was tryin' to get an idea of who had young cattle to sell. I know a person up north who might be lookin' for some stock."

The man's eyes were hard as iron. "Not here. Everything's spoken for."

"Oh, then I won't trouble you. Nice place you've got here, though."

"Save your breath. We're sellin' the whole works and goin' back to Indiana."

"I'm sorry if things haven't gone well."

"You don't know what to be sorry for."

"I'm sure I don't, but I apologize for the bother."

"Don't mention it."

Dearing turned his horse around, led it out, and swung aboard. On his way down the lane, he stopped where the boy was looking after the goat. "What's your goat's name?"

"Queenie."

"That's a good name. She's a nice-looking goat."

The boy squinted. "Thanks."

"I talked with your neighbor. Sounds like they're pullin' out."

"Yeah. Their girl died. They don't want to be here anymore."

"I'm sorry to hear that. What was her name?"

"Carrie."

"Pretty sad. I can understand why they're bitter."

"They say no one wants to do anything."

"Why would that be?"

"I don't know. Scared, I guess. My pa says to stay out of it. He hates cowpunchers."

"Your pa does?"

"No, Mitch Redmond. My pa does ranch work."

"No harm in that. Well, I'd better move along. Take good care of your goat."

"Thanks. I like your horse."

"Thanks to you."

Dearing rode into Burnett at nightfall. He did not have a plan beyond staying for the night, so he put his horse in the livery stable and arranged to sleep there for another two bits. The owner said he would tell the night man so he would know, and Dearing went off to find something to eat.

After an inexpensive meal of beef stew, he found his way to the Buckskin Saloon. As night was drawing in, he told himself he would have one beer and go back to the stable. He took his place at the bar, ordered his drink, and paid for it. Only a couple of other patrons stood at the bar, and Dearing did not expect much merrymaking on a Wednesday night.

A young fellow with his hat tipped back and his spurs jingling came striding in. He passed behind Dearing and stopped about ten feet to Dearing's left. He clinked a silver dollar on the bar and called for whiskey. When the bartender served him, he asked where the women were. The bartender said they were still putting on their powder.

Dearing returned his attention to his drink, and as he did so, he caught a glance at the mirror that sent a jolt to his stomach. Trent Malone appeared behind him like a dark cloud. The man stood there for a long moment with his brows drawn and his eyes glaring. When he turned and walked farther into the saloon, Dearing saw that he was not alone. A shorter man in a light-colored hat and duster walked beside him. They stalked past the boisterous young fellow, who had gone quiet, and they stopped at the bar long enough to toss down a shot of whiskey. With a shuffle of feet and then a measured tread, they passed in back of Dearing and out into the night.

Dearing settled as a long breath eased out of him. He would have expected Malone to be at the ranch, with Wilmer and Endicott, in the routine of that world. But here he was, on the prowl, with the ill-humored Dowd at his side. In a way, the two made sense together, as if the lesser one had found a benefactor. Dearing wondered if he had gotten hired on at the ranch.

Dearing contracted his shoulders and shivered to drive away the chill. He had not expected to come back to something like this. The town had seemed dull and uneventful as always when he rode in, but that illusion had vanished. He felt as if he had an evil spirit hunched and clinging onto the back of his neck.

His first thought was to go to the stable, gather his horse, and leave. But he knew that was no good. He had come all this way to see if he could do something, and he had to spend the night at least. Keeping an eye on the mirror, he finished his beer. The pleasant taste was gone, and he had no interest in another glass.

The night man was on duty when Dearing returned to the livery stable. He found the old man in the harness room, sitting by a cast-iron stove with no fire in it. A lantern hung from a rafter hook, casting a glow on the burlap sack that the old man was mending.

"So you came back, huh?"

"I don't know for how long."

"Well, you're here. Have a seat. Tell me what's new." O'Connor pointed at a wooden crate.

Dearing sat down amidst the clutter. A pile of burlap bags lay on the floor near his feet. Ropes and straps and broken reins and short lengths of chain hung on nails along the walls. A singletree lay on a grain box near O'Connor's chair.

"Not much new," said Dearing. "I went off and worked at another place for a while. Decided to stop here on my way through."

"Might as well."

"I thought roundup might have started by now."

"Couple of more days."

"Not that I'm lookin' for work, but I guess Rich Farrow has a full crew."

"Can't say. That is, I don't know for sure. That fella Endicott left. Farrow put on another fella that came in. Other than that, I don't know."

Dearing nodded. He hoped Malone and Dowd were riding back to the ranch at that moment.

O'Connor drew a pint bottle out of his coat pocket and held it beside his lap. "Hope you don't mind."

"No. Go ahead."

The old man unscrewed the cap, wiped his hand across the

mouth of the bottle, and took a sip. As he put the cap on, he frowned. "These don't last very long. I thought I had more than that."

"Don't worry on my account."

"I won't." The old man shrugged and put the bottle away. He moved his shoulders around and took up the needle and thread.

Dearing spoke in a lowered voice. "I happened to go past the Redmond place today. I understand they're selling out."

"I heard that, too. Can't blame 'em."

Dearing sat without speaking as the night man sewed with the large needle and coarse thread. The needle went through the loose weave of the burlap with no trouble, and the man did not take pains to make a fine, even stitch. When he came to the end, he tied off with a couple of loops and reached for an open knife that lay on the grain box next to the singletree. He cut the thread, put the knife back, and turned the sack over to expose another hole. He tied a knot in the double thread and went to work on the torn fabric.

Dearing observed the singletree. It was about two and a half feet long, with a clevis ring in the middle and an iron shackle and hook on each end. He thought there might be some import in the night man keeping such an item within arm's reach.

Keeping his voice low, Dearing said, "I had the impression that he was bitter about his daughter."

"Like I say, I can't blame him."

"Has no one done anything?"

The old man shrugged. "Not that I know."

"Are people afraid?"

"Could be."

"Is that why Endicott took off?"

"He left not long after you did."

Dearing pondered. "Huh. Who else?"

"Who else left?"

"No. Who else is afraid?"

"Don't ask me."

Dearing let out a long breath. "I thought you knew something."

"It's hard to know anything for sure."

Lowering his voice almost to a whisper, Dearing said, "Look. I think you know something. And I think you wish someone could do something."

The old man took a few seconds to answer. "Maybe you're right."

"You help the barber once in a while to bring a body in, don't you?"

The stableman shrugged again. "Maybe I do."

"And I wonder if you helped him on this occasion."

The old eyes held steady, and the old voice came low. "Maybe I did."

"And I have a hunch the barber saw something when he was preparing the body for burial. Something he thought you should both stay mum about."

"You're comin' pretty close, boy. I don't know how much anyone wants to let go."

Dearing deliberated. He could not make himself say the words "with child," and he felt that any more direct wording, or reference to details that would lead to that conclusion, would be invading the privacy of a person he never knew. So he left it at that and took another tack. "It's not as if no one has an idea of who it was, is it?"

"I couldn't say."

Dearing thought it through. Endicott had made himself scarce, just as it seemed Dearing had done. The barber was afraid for his life, and the stableman did not want to give him away.

O'Connor ran about twenty stitches and ended with a seam

like the previous one. He had just enough thread to tie it off, and he cut it with the knife. With the bag still in his lap, he took out the bottle and finished the remainder.

"There's a dead soldier," he said, turning the bottle so that it caught the light. He tipped it each way and set it on the grain box. "It's very disagreeable to run out so early in the shift."

Dearing thought he caught a hint. "I'm here for the night," he said. "I could skip out and get you another one, and I could sit up and chin a while longer, just to pass the time."

The night man pursed his lips. "That's kind of you. I wouldn't turn it down. I'll see about gettin' a fire goin' in the stove while you're gone."

Dearing buttoned his coat and put on his gloves as he walked out into the night. It was the third week of May, but nights were still chilly. The last frost of the season might be yet to come.

The interior of the saloon seemed bright by comparison. A half dozen patrons stood along the bar, and their voices were indistinct. Dearing ordered a pint of whiskey, paid with a dollar, and waited for change. The bartender wrapped the bottle in newspaper, slid it flat across the bar, and handed Dearing a quarter. Dearing took hold of the package and turned around, intending to head for the door, but he stopped short to avoid running into a woman wearing a pink stole and a straw hat with black feathers.

"I have a place where you can drink that," she said.

"It's for someone else."

"Everyone says that."

"Well, it's the truth." He still held the quarter he had taken in change. "Here," he said, handing it to her. "Get something for yourself."

She gave a small pout. "Thanks. Come again when you can stay longer."

He wanted to tell her that everyone said that, but he thought better of it and said, "I'll try." He slipped the package into his right coat pocket and put on his gloves as he walked out into the dark night. He was glad not to have seen Malone or Dowd, and he hoped again that they were on their way to the ranch.

He crossed the street and walked the three blocks to the livery stable. As he went in through the walk-through door, he saw that something was different. No light came from the harness room, and a lit lantern, perhaps the same one he had seen earlier, was shedding light where it sat on a bench near a stall. Dearing wondered if the night man was puttering around.

"Say, Wim," he called out as he took off his gloves and put them in his empty pocket. Getting no answer, he picked up the lantern and walked through the open door of the harness room.

Something large was out of place. Dearing recognized it as the midsection of a man, but it was at eye level. Trying to make sense of it, he raised the lantern, to be met with the grotesque sight of a purple face and crooked head. The slouch hat had fallen off, but there was no mistaking that it was Wim O'Connor hanging from a rafter.

A surge of panic ran through Dearing's skull, down through his neck and shoulders, and out through his body. Before he could form a thought, a blow between his shoulder blades drove most of the breath out of him. He dropped the lantern and stumbled into the body, which gave way.

As he gained his balance, he felt a strap tighten around his neck. He raised his hands and dug at the leather, which had the thickness of a bridle rein, but he could not move it. He felt it tighten, and his tongue went out of his mouth as he felt pressure build in his eyes. He kicked his feet out in front of him and dropped straight down, breaking the hold. As he scrambled onto all fours, the upward-slanting light showed him the shadowed face of Trent Malone, his features locked in an expression of hatred as he searched for a way to finish what he had started. Posting his weight on his left foot, Malone kicked with his right and caught Dearing in the ribs. As he positioned himself to kick again, Dearing pulled himself up by the lip of the grain box and laid his hand on one end of the singletree.

Malone was repositioning himself when Dearing leaned forward and swung the singletree, catching Malone behind the ear with the iron shackle.

Malone had been drawing a gun, and he fired a wild shot as his head jerked to one side and his hat tumbled away.

Dearing grabbed for the lantern where it lay, but he had to let it go. The lens had broken, and flames were spreading on the lantern as well as on a pile of burlap bags. With the help of the dancing flames, however, he could see that Malone was done for.

Voices sounded, and men came running. One man had a lantern, and another carried a rifle. Two more bunched up behind them. They all held still for a few seconds until the man with the rifle held Dearing in place and gave orders. The others went to work. Two men cut the rope and lowered the body, while the fourth man, whom Dearing recognized as the barber, carried water and put out the fire.

The group re-formed in the open area of the stable, outside the harness room. A couple of more men had arrived, and a second lantern hung from a post. Two more men came in with pistols drawn and a shrinking Dawson Dowd between them.

"This one was holding horses out by the corral."

The man with the rifle ran his eyes around the room, lowered them to the two bodies, and came back to Dearing. "What can you tell us?"

"I had been visiting with the night man, and I went to buy him a pint of whiskey. When I came back, I found him where you did. Before I could do anything, this fellow Malone came up behind me and tried to strangle me. I was lucky to fetch him one on the head before he could fire a straight shot."

The man with the rifle grimaced. "I think I might have heard this Malone's name mentioned, but why would he want to do this to the old man?"

Dearing blinked his eyes. "I'm sorry it happened to him. He knew something. He didn't tell me straight out, but Malone must have been listening."

"What did he know?"

"The barber can tell you. It has to do with why Malone would have had a reason to kill the Redmond girl."

All eyes turned to the barber. He swallowed hard and said, "I think that could very well be the case." He lowered his eyes to the spot where the night man lay. "That is, yes, he knew something."

★ ★ ★ ★ ★

BUCKSKIN RUBY

★ ★ ★ ★ ★

I was hauling water with my donkey named Smoke when a stranger rode up to the work camp. He was riding a buckskin horse and wore a hat that matched the color of his horse and the color of his fringed buckskin shirt. He had dark, flowing hair that came down over his ears and touched his collar, and he wore a wine-colored neckerchief. As he stepped his horse from one side to another, I saw that he wore a ruby ring.

He smiled and looked down at me with flashing dark eyes. "Who's in charge of hiring on this project?"

"Either of the Putnam brothers," I said. "They're out on the job right now, but I expect they'll come in for noon dinner."

"That's good." The sun glinted off of his ruby as he put his hands on the saddle horn and leaned forward. "What's your name, kid?"

"Benny."

"Is this your donkey?"

"Yes, he's mine."

"Are you on your own, then?"

"Yes, sir. I am."

His eyes swept over me. "Kind of young."

"I'm fourteen."

"I didn't mean there was anything wrong with it."

I shrugged. "If you want to water your horse, it's all right. I'm going to empty this water into the tank." I pointed at the two ten-gallon barrels lashed to the packsaddle on my donkey.

The newcomer pushed his hat back on his head. "Thanks, but I watered him before we crossed the creek. That's Little Hat Creek, isn't it?"

"Yes, it is."

"And this is the Little Hat ditch project."

"That's right."

"Is it named after a little hat? The creek, that is."

"No. Little Hat Creek is named after Hat Creek, which it flows into, like the Little Laramie River flows into the Laramie River."

"That's good to know." The stranger put on a routine smile and glanced around. "I imagine the Putnam brothers would like to get as much work done as possible before the cold weather sets in and the ground freezes."

"I couldn't say."

"Oh, I know. I'll ask them if they're hiring."

I caught a glance at the man's rope tied next to his saddle horn. He looked more like a cowpuncher than a ditch grader to me, but at that point in my life I was too young to have much of an opinion about things.

I poured the water into the tank for the mules and horses and led my donkey across the sagebrush flat to the creek. Now in the latter half of September, patches of yellow leaves were showing in the cottonwood trees along the creek bottom. The chokecherry bushes were changing color as well, from dark green to shades of yellow, pink, and red. The weather had been hot and dry for weeks, but a cool wind blew from the northwest.

I untied the bucket from the top of the pack and went to work dipping water out of the creek and pouring it into the barrels. I poured a bucketful into one side and then a bucketful into the other, back and forth, to keep the weight balanced for Smoke.

The Putnam brothers had returned to camp when Smoke and I came trailing in with two more barrels of water. The brothers sat on their three-legged folding stools in the shade of their tent. As usual, they were dressed alike, wearing hats with peaked crowns and flat round brims, vests of light brown wool, white work shirts with long sleeves, grey striped pants, and stovepipe boots with mule-ear pull straps. The brothers had light brown hair and mustaches, high cheekbones, suntanned faces, and sturdy chests and shoulders. Vic, the older of the two, was a few pounds heavier than Ned. They each lifted a hand to wave at me as I led my donkey past them.

By the time I had the water poured into the stock tank, Gilliam had rung the triangle. The Putnam brothers served themselves first, and the newcomer followed. The brothers had their stools set in the chuck area, as it was their custom to eat with the men and chat with them. The newcomer in the buckskin shirt took a seat on the ground and was eating beefsteak from a tin plate in his lap.

The work crew had not come in yet, so I didn't have to wait in line. I picked up a plate and utensils from the tailgate of the chuck wagon and served myself fried meat and potatoes from the cast-iron skillets at the edge of the fire. Gilliam, the cook and ruler of the chuck wagon, stood by in a white shirt and apron, smoothing his clipped white mustache. His helper, a boy named Garry who limped, held out a tin plate of biscuits for me to help myself.

I sat cross-legged on the ground near the newcomer.

"I'm off to a good start," he said. "Made it just in time for the dinner bell."

"That's good," I said. "They feed us well here."

"By the way." He paused with his knife and fork. "My name's

Bill. Bill Smith. I didn't tell you my name when you told me yours."

Vic Putnam spoke up. "Benny's our Mexican." When no one said anything, he added, "But he's a good one."

Bill spoke to me again. "It's a nice donkey you've got."

"Thanks. We get along just fine."

Bill went to work driving a scraper, and according to what the other men said at suppertime, he picked up the technique right away and had a good hand with horses he hadn't worked with before.

He had changed into a drab flannel work shirt before he went out for the afternoon, so he did not look so flashy as he sat on the ground and ate a bowl of stew. The breeze did not die down at sunset, so most of the men went to the bunkhouse tent when they finished eating. Bill made short work of his meal and joined them.

I followed not far behind. When I found a chair in the bunkhouse, Bill was chatting it up with the other men and handling a deck of cards. He cracked the deck, shuffled it, cut it, and showed the ace of spades. A couple of men laughed. He went through the motions again and showed the queen of hearts. Men laughed as before.

As he worked the deck, the ruby ring on his left hand sparkled in the lamplight. I realized he had handled his spoon, and his knife earlier, with his left hand. I could tell he enjoyed attention as he set the deck of cards down with a flourish and began to roll a cigarette.

"How are you at flipping a coin?" asked one of the men.

"No good." Bill shook tobacco grains into the trough he made of the cigarette paper. "I can flip the coin and catch it all right, but I can't tell whether it'll come up heads or tails."

Morg Salter, the foreman, said, "No one can."

Bill shrugged. "Some people claim to be able to. They use a heavy coin, and they say they can count the turns or flips it takes. I don't have that good of an eye."

Salter said again, "No one can."

Bill raised his eyebrows. "I didn't say they could." He licked the paper, tapped the seam, and popped a match. He lit the cigarette and rolled it to the side of his mouth without touching it, then shook out the match and tossed it in a sardine can. "But we can try."

He reached into his pocket and drew out a silver dollar. "Now this is heavy, and you can make it turn slow." He flipped it up with his left hand, watched it make its slow revolutions, and let it fall flat in his right hand. "But I wasn't able to count the turns." He flipped it again, slow like before. "Can anyone else?" No one answered. He flipped it higher, and everyone watched it go up, spinning. It came down flat. "Now that's the deal, as everyone knows. The higher you toss it, the faster it comes down. So if you're goin' to try to keep your eye on it, you want to toss it not too high and not flick it too hard with your thumb." He did as he said, and the coin took a lazy, rotating climb in the air and turned only once as it came down to fall flat in his palm. "Even at that, I couldn't count the turns. But some people might."

Salter said, "What I meant was, nobody can predict it. You've got a fifty-fifty chance every time, and even if it comes up tails a dozen times in a row, it still has the same chance the next time as any other time."

"Sure," said Bill. "Everyone knows that, or should." He took out a five-dollar gold piece, spun it up into the air, swiped it with his right hand, and slapped it on the back of his left hand. "It's all chance, and the same chance every time, like you say. That's why a fella shouldn't bet on it, though people do."

"You sound like a gambler. I heard you tell someone you

might set up a business. Is that it—a gamblin' business?"

"I didn't say I wanted to set up a business. I said that if I ever did go into business, I would deal in dry goods so my inventory didn't go to spoil. But that was because we were talking about the weather to begin with."

"So you're not going to engage men in games of chance?"

"Not at all. If I play a game, it's a game of skill."

Salter spoke in something like a drawl as he said, "Where I come from, men have skills for things like ropin' steers."

Bill shrugged. "I've done that."

"Easy to say, when you don't have to prove it."

Bill shot out a small puff of smoke. "I have my rope. You get some ropin' stock, and I'll try my hand against yours."

"Hah," said Salter. "We can get along without steers or calves. We can rope this kid's donkey."

I felt a sinking in the pit of my stomach.

Bill said, "No need to pick on the donkey."

"Aw, hell, it won't hurt him. They're so thickheaded anyway. Back home, a lot of fellas practice ropin' donkeys."

Bill took a drag on his cigarette. "I'll let the kid speak for himself."

My heart was thumping in my throat, and I felt a dizziness, but I had to talk. "I'd rather you didn't. I don't care if it doesn't hurt him. I just don't want you to."

Salter said, "It's all in fun. Just to get this fella to put up some proof. He talks a good game."

"I don't want you to."

Bill spit a fleck of tobacco and said, "If this boy doesn't want you to, nobody should try to make him agree to it. If you want to see if I can handle a rope, you can watch me in the morning. I'll rope out any workhorses that play hard to get when it comes time to hitch 'em up."

Salter stood up and walked out of the bunkhouse. I assumed

he went to the Putnam brothers' tent, as he sometimes did in the evening. Everyone knew they kept a whiskey bottle, even though it was against the rules for anyone else to have liquor in camp.

The evening air around the campfire was warmer after supper the next night, so most of the men lingered by the fire. So did the Putnam brothers. A thin little mouse-haired fellow named Marcus, who worked with a shovel every day, had brought out his four-string guitar and was singing songs about the girl back home, the girl who married another, the girl who died from the chilling night air, and so on. When he came to a rest, he asked if anyone else would like to hear a song or even sing one.

Bill, who had been listening and singing along, said, "I've got one or two I wouldn't mind trying."

"Would you like to use the guitar?"

"If you don't mind."

"Not at all." Marcus reached over and handed him the instrument.

After a minute or so of strumming and tuning, Bill sang a song about a girl who twined flowers into her raven-dark hair. She spoke of lilies and roses and myrtle of an emerald hue. The story ended with her being abandoned and heartbroken, with visions of love all faded away.

After a faint applause, Bill said, "The other one I'll sing is called 'My Pretty Quadroon.' " He strummed again, hit a rhythm, and sang a song about a slave who loved a girl named Cora. She had cheeks like the wild rose of June, but the master fancied her, so he sold the slave far away to the rice fields. Then the girl died, and the man ended his story looking forward to seeing her in heaven.

A strange silence seemed to have fallen around the campfire. No one applauded. I didn't know if it was because the song was so sad, or so different from everyone else's lives, or if it was something I didn't understand. Vic Putnam had an expression on his face as if he had swallowed a dose of iron. For my part, I did not clap because I did not think I had enough authority to do it on my own.

Garry, the kitchen boy, did not have as much hesitation. He said, "What's a quadroon?"

Gilliam twisted his mouth and pulled on his trimmed white mustache. He said, "It means she was one-quarter Negro."

"Oh."

Bill held out the guitar.

As Marcus took it back, he said, "I never heard that song before."

"One among many you hear in the various places you go." Bill grimaced in the firelight. "But there's very few that I know well enough to play a couple of chords and sing."

Bill and three other workers were lagging pennies after supper the next evening as the sun slipped behind the mountains. They were laughing and joking and having a good time as they lost and won a few pennies. I was sitting with my back to the tent, feeling the warmth of the canvas and enjoying the last of the sunlight.

As the men took their places at the lag line for another round, Morg Salter appeared. Well-built and a little taller than average, he wore his hat at a jaunty angle and had his sleeves folded up. He had muscular arms, and I thought he flexed his muscle as he held his pipe at the corner of his mouth.

He blew out a cloud of smoke and spoke to Bill. "Do you ever do anything more manly than pitch pennies and cut cards?"

Bill smiled. "Depends on the occasion."

"Different camps have their traditions. Contests and matches. All in fun, you know."

Bill raised his eyebrows. "I've seen some of it. In a mining camp, I had the pleasure of watching and hearing a cussing contest. They used mules for judges."

"That's cute."

"And in other camps they have wood-chopping, and barrel-rolling. I've even seen spoon races, where they run holding an egg in a spoon—and that's in places where an egg is worth a dollar."

"At this camp, sometimes we have boxing matches."

"Is that right?"

Salter's drawl came out. "All civilized. We use boxing gloves, so no one gets hurt."

"I see. Is this some kind of an initiation?"

"Not always. Sometimes it's just a friendly challenge." Salter blew out another puff of smoke. "Are you up for it?"

Bill's glance swept over the other man. "Is that a challenge from you, then?"

Salter gave a wide smile. "That's how it's meant." He turned to me. "Benny, go into the back of the tent, to the gear box, and bring out the two pair of gloves. You know the ones I mean."

I nodded. I had a picture of them in my mind. I stood up from my chair and walked into the tent, where the mixed smells of dust and leather and sweaty clothes hung in the warm air. I headed to the far end and opened a large wooden box that held ropes and stakes and a wooden block and tackle, along with burlap bags, folded canvas sheets, a singletree for hanging animals, and two pairs of boxing gloves.

The gloves were large and well padded, with a covering of soft, reddish leather. I had seen them come out of the box before, so I knew them on sight. I gathered the four gloves into my arms, lowered the lid, and made my way outside.

Bill and Salter stood waiting with their hats off. As I handed two gloves to each of them, Salter looked down his nose at

Bill's hands.

"You might want to take off your ring. You can hurt your finger."

"I don't take it off."

"Suit yourself."

I tied the laces for both men, and they stepped away to face off. Bill held his gloves at chest level with his elbows relaxed. Salter held his gloves at about the same level but made small, circular motions as if he was trying to draw in his opponent.

Bill stepped forward, jabbed with his left hand, hit Salter's joined gloves, and sank back. He began to move to his right, circling, and Salter moved along with him. Salter made sniffing sounds as he continued to make small motions with his gloves. Bill jabbed again, glanced a blow off of Salter's gloves, and stepped back.

Salter had his face tight and his eyes intent, and he moved in a slow, methodical way.

Bill changed his style. He still circled to his right, but he dropped his gloves to his hips and danced from one foot to the other. Now he jabbed with his right hand, which seemed to throw Salter off. Bill changed his footing, jabbed with his left, then danced and jabbed with his right.

Salter fended him off. Bill sank back, bounded from one foot to another, stepped forward with a right punch, and followed with a great left-handed roundhouse from below waist level. It was prodigious. It knocked Salter back on his heels, and as he tried to get his footing, he fell to the ground.

Bill stood in place with the large gloves a little below chest level. He watched Salter as the man rose to one elbow, sat up, rolled to the side, and pushed himself up onto his feet.

"Are you all right?" said Bill.

Salter moved his head back and forth. "Yeah. I'm fine."

"Is that enough, or do you want to go some more?"

"I think it's enough for today."

"All in fun, of course, like you said."

"Sure." Salter held his wrists toward me, and I stepped forward to untie the laces and pull off the gloves.

Bill stood waiting, so I turned around to do the same for him. As I did so, I saw the Putnam brothers about ten yards back, not far from the front of their tent. I assumed they had watched the match. Now that it was over and their foreman was finding his hat and pipe, they turned and walked into their tent. A minute later, Salter joined them.

As I pulled the second glove off of Bill, he said, "Thanks, Benny. Maybe you'll make a referee someday." When I did not answer, he said, "You'd probably rather work with your donkey."

I said, "For right now, anyway."

Bill and his pals were lagging pennies again the next day as Garry, Gilliam, and I got the water ready for men to take baths. The day being Saturday and a market day in town, the crew had quit at noon, and some of the men who were going into town wanted to bathe first. Our method was not very complicated, and it allowed men to clean up in a short amount of time and not use much water.

The bath area was set up several yards away from camp, so that the mud would not become a nuisance. The men had put up a canvas wall with poles and ropes, and the man bathing stood in a tub with his back to everyone else.

I hauled the water from the creek and stood by as Gilliam heated it in large pots over the fire. I dipped the warm water and handed it to Garry, who swung the bucket with his limp as he carried it, then splashed the water in trickles on the man who stood in the tub. When the man was done, he stepped out of the tub onto a wooden pallet, dried himself, and put on his clothes.

When Gilliam called Bill's name, Bill came striding to the bath area and took his clothes off in his carefree manner. From where I stood, midway between the fire and the bath area, I had a clear view of Bill's bare back side, down to his ankle, where a number was tattooed in blue ink.

At that time, I did not know much about the larger world, but I knew that some men who were marked in that way had been in prison, just as convicts and slaves, in earlier times, had been burned in the hand. At this moment, I knew that others had seen the tattoo on Bill's ankle, and I also knew that as a general practice in the West, people did not ask a man about his past.

A few men set off for town on horseback, and a few rode in the wagon with Gilliam and his helper, Garry. The Putnam brothers had left earlier, and we were given to understand that they would stay at the hotel and have baths there. I rode my donkey bareback, poking along a ways behind the wagon. In a little while, Bill caught up with me on his buckskin horse and fell in alongside.

He was dressed the way he was when he first rode into the work camp. In addition to his regular felt hat, he wore his buckskin shirt, maroon-colored neckerchief, and denim trousers. He also had put on a gunbelt I had not noticed before. He must have seen me look at it, for he said, "Nothin' to worry about. Just a precaution."

"There's usually not much trouble in Belden," I said.

"That's good. There's too much trouble in the world, and it's too easy to fall into."

"I stay away from it."

"It's a good way to be. And of course there's different kinds." As we rode on by ourselves, he said, "I was in trouble once, with the law. It cost me my future with a girl. She had to let me go, and I couldn't blame her. I felt as if I didn't deserve her, wasn't good enough for her, after that. It's a bad way to feel, and it's hard to fix. Much better to avoid it if you can, and not get in trouble in the first place."

I thought he might be giving me this wholesome advice because he knew I had seen the tattoo on his ankle, but he seemed sincere, in a big-brother kind of way, which was more than most men bothered with, in my experience. After all, I was just a Mexican kid with a donkey, in a world of white men who liked to drink and swagger and flex their muscles and talk about the private parts of women. I did not think Bill fit that pattern, but I did not know how much he might change if he had a few drinks in town.

Market day in late September brought a great many people into town from the surrounding country. Folks were selling produce out of their wagons—brown potatoes, white turnips, red beets, orange pumpkins, and yellow corn with light green husks. Lambs and goats bleated, and calves bawled. Chickens cackled in crates. Dogs loitered, and little nester kids ran in and out among the wagons, chasing and giggling.

Bill asked me what I was going to do, and I told him that on trips like this, I watched the men's horses while they spent their time in the saloon.

He said, "I'd like you to watch my horse, too."

He dismounted in front of the telegraph office, and I slid off of my donkey. Bill handed me a two-bit piece and said, "I need to go in here for a few minutes. Then I'll cross over to the saloon, too."

I waited for more than a few minutes. When he came out, we crossed the street and he handed me the reins again. "Do those other fellas give you anything?"

"Sometimes a ginger beer or a stick of licorice, but I don't

151

mind the little bit of work. It gives me something to do."

"Well, if you get tired of standing in one place, you can walk my horse up and down the street. But I don't expect to spend a long time in there, anyway."

I stood in the street with Smoke and the buckskin and watched the activity around me. In the empty lot between the saloon and the hotel, two pairs of men were pitching horseshoes. In the other empty lots, as well as in the street, people were selling garden crops and farm animals, as I had already seen. I wondered what else might be on sale, so I wandered down the street, leading Bill's horse with one hand and Smoke with the other.

I paused in front of a two-wheeled shay where a man had an assortment of knives and razors. I saw a couple of pocketknives the likes of which I would like to have after I saved up a little more money.

The man asked me, "Where'd you get that nice horse, boy?"

"I'm watching it for a man."

"It's not for trade, then."

"No."

I walked on, passing a butcher's cart that had a canvas canopy put up. The proprietor had a long fan that he was waving to keep the flies off the cuts of meat. It looked as if he had lamb and pork, not the darker shades of beef. One object caught my attention. Suspended above the meat, hanging on a meat hook from the wooden frame above, a set of heart and lungs was darkening and drying in the afternoon air.

The man said, "Don't get too close, boy. Those animals draw flies."

I walked on.

When I returned to the saloon, men were still pitching horseshoes in the empty lot. The colors of Bill's buckskin shirt and ruby-colored neckerchief caught my eye. He was talking to

a long-haired, bearded man who looked like a hunter or trapper. Horseshoes clanked on the iron stakes, and I could see that
a game was under way with two men at one end and their
partners at the other. The man who looked like a trapper was
talking loud, and I gathered that he and his partner, at the other
end, were taking on other teams for a dollar a game. Bill said he
did not have a partner but enjoyed playing the game as well as
watching it.

At that moment, the Putnam brothers crossed in front of me.
The smell of bath soap carried on the air, and I imagined they
had come from the hotel. They observed Bill as they walked by.

The man talking to Bill turned and called out, "Hey, you fellas look like a couple of sports. Why don't you come over and
try your luck?" As he raised his voice, he had the tone of a man
who had had something to drink.

The Putnam brothers stopped. Vic said, "We don't play that
game."

The man laughed in his beard. "You're a couple of big bugs,
then, aren't you?"

Vic said, "Watch who you talk to that way, mister."

"Bah. You sound like you got somethin' in your ass."

"You'll find out if I do." Vic handed his hat and vest to his
brother. He marched over a few paces, and without coming to a
stop, he punched the man in the jaw.

The bearded man dropped the horseshoe he was holding and
came back with a heavy fist on Vic's cheekbone.

The fight was on, and the stranger held his own against Vic
Putnam, who I had assumed would be hard to beat. The two
traded punches until Vic grabbed the man's hair and pulled.
The man flailed his arm and settled it around Vic's neck, breaking Vic's hold and throwing him to the ground, where his white
shirt picked up dirt and bits of grass.

The bearded man stood back, waiting for Vic to get up, when

Ned Putnam attacked the man from behind. He clobbered the man with his heavy fists, and when the man went down on all fours, Ned kicked him in the ribs.

By now, the man's partner had come running from the other end of the horseshoe game, and he flew at Ned with both knees raised and doubled. Like a projectile, he hit Ned in the back and flattened him.

A sharp voice carried from the board sidewalk in front of the saloon. "Hold it right there, or I'll shoot someone."

All eyes turned to Morg Salter, who held a six-gun leveled.

The man who had landed on Ned scrambled around and stood up. "And who the hell are you?"

"My name's Morgan Salter, and I'm the foreman for these two men you attacked."

"I don't even know them, but they came up and started trouble with my partner."

Salter spoke in his drawl. "Takes two sides to make a fight. And I'm here to end it. So stand back."

The man did as he was told. His partner crawled toward him, and with help, he made it to his feet.

The Putnam brothers stood up and brushed themselves off. Vic said, "He started it with his smart talk."

Salter motioned with his head toward Bill. "Did he have anything to do with it?"

Vic shook his head. "Not that I saw."

Salter put his six-gun in his holster. "Good thing for him." The foreman's eyes wandered around and landed on me. "What are you doing?"

"I'm watching his horse."

"Why aren't you watching the others?"

"I was getting around to it, but he paid me to watch his."

Salter's eyes rolled up as if he was reading something on his hat brim. He took a breath and brought his gaze around to me.

"You're lucky you stayed out of the trouble. But you should keep farther away."

I didn't like him finding fault with me. I said, "I was just standing here. I didn't know there was going to be any trouble."

"No one ever does."

The men set up the bath area again the next Saturday, as another market day was scheduled in town. A well-known boot company from Kansas had announced that it would be there, and a hat company had sent out similar word. As before, the Putnam brothers left camp ahead of everyone else, and I imagined they hoped for a fresh bath that would last a little longer than the previous one.

To my surprise, Bill made ready to leave not long after the bosses did. He did not seem to be in a hurry, and I did not expect that he had any plans to overtake them. I said goodbye to him and decided to ride in the wagon with the cook and his helper.

Almost everyone on the crew went into town this time. Two of the men who had reputations as penny-pinchers stayed behind to watch the stock. Even the two young fellows who worked as day and night herders had the chance to go, and as the bosses had paid everyone through the day before, a general mood of cheerfulness floated on the air.

The ride into town was slow and bouncy, but the weather was fair. The sun was shining, and a light breeze came from the northwest—not bad for the first day of October, when anything could happen from stuffy heat to cold rain to wet snow.

As we rolled into town, the streets were lined with people selling goods as before. One new detail presented itself—a low speaker's platform or stage had been dragged into place in the lot between the hotel and the saloon, and a hand-painted sign sat on an easel. It said: *Public Event at 4:00 p.m.*

From the position of the sun, I guessed the hour to be about three o'clock, so I had time to look at the boots and hats and still take a place near the stage. I wondered if there was going to be music, humor, or some kind of speech. The last time I had seen an outdoor presentation, it had been a poetry declamation by a man who claimed to be following in the footsteps of "the great Hoosier Poet," whose name I did not recognize. The time before, it had been the Bremen Town Musicians. So I did not know what to expect.

The boots and hats were way out of my range, so I did not spend much time coveting them. Back at the stage, I found a place near the front as a crowd began to gather. After a while, as I looked over each shoulder, I guessed about forty or fifty people were present.

I heard people chat among themselves and ask one another the time. At a little before four o'clock, a man stepped out of the hotel. I recognized him by his buckskin shirt and scarlet neckerchief. He was also wearing his gunbelt. He kept his eyes straight ahead as he walked to the stage and stepped up onto it. He turned, gazed over the crowd, and spoke.

"Good afternoon, folks. I'm glad to see you all here. I have some information I would like to present, and I leave it to the good citizens of this county to decide what to do."

A man near me in a cattleman's hat spoke up. "What kind of information? You make it sound like it might be something criminal."

Bill nodded. "You've got a pretty good idea, sir. It's about something that happened a while back, a long ways away but still here in Laramie County, and it entails someone among us."

A murmur ran through the crowd, and a voice rose up from off to the right side. Morg Salter said, "Who are you to be talking about a criminal? There's several of us here that have a hunch that you've been in jail."

"What's your name?" asked the cattleman.

Salter said, "He calls himself Bill Smith. He could just as well be Jim Jones."

Bill held his palms up. "It's true that I gave my name as Bill Smith when I came to work here for the Putnam brothers." He paused, and several people in the crowd turned to regard the brothers, who stood with their foreman. Bill went on. "My real name is Bill Underwood, and you can check up on me. It's true that I've been in jail. But that doesn't keep me from telling the truth."

A man in a Scotch cap said, "Well, let's get on with it. It's going to get dark in a couple of hours."

Salter said, "I don't know why we need to listen to him."

Bill turned his palms up. "No one has to. But some people might find it interesting."

Another wave of muttering went through the crowd, and Bill cleared his throat.

He spoke in a raised voice. "There's a story I came here to tell." He paused as the crowd gave him its attention. "It began about fifteen years ago, down in Cheyenne. A girl I knew was taken advantage of, or to put it more strongly, violated, and then strangled. I was behind bars at the time. She had turned me down because of the trouble I had gotten into—robbing a train, for those who are interested—and she had become engaged to another young man. Whoever killed her killed him as well, and it was speculated that two people committed the crime."

"How long were you in jail?" asked Salter.

"Ten years. When I got out, I learned that the crime had never been solved, so I went about looking into it myself." He paused as the crowd gave him full attention. "One of the early details I learned was that the girl had not been wearing, and did not have in her effects, a piece of jewelry I had given her. That gave me something to look for."

The man in the Scotch cap said, "What kind of jewelry was it?"

Bill glanced from one side to the other as he took in the audience. "It was a gold medallion with a ruby set in it, and on the back it had an expression engraved in Latin. *Amor vincit omnia.*"

I stole a look at the Putnam brothers, and they both wore faces of stone.

Bill continued. "The murders happened in Cheyenne, as I said, about fifteen years ago. At that time, men were working on the Sybille Ditch project, and some of them did their carousing in Cheyenne." He paused. "The piece of jewelry turned up in Laramie twelve years later, at the time that men were working on the Wheatland Reservoir. It was given to a girl who lived in Laramie."

The faces of the Putnam brothers had grown harder, and I thought I saw a glow of resentment on both of them.

The man in the Scotch cap said, "This is all a good story, but where is the jewelry, and where is the girl it was given to?"

Bill raised his eyebrows. "I have the medallion and the chain that went with it. The girl is here in town."

A collection of gasps and exclamations went up. Bill held out his hands to quiet the crowd. "Not to delay any more, I have an assistant who can bring the young woman here." He lowered his gaze. "Blanche."

A woman with greying brown hair and the thickness of middle age, who was dressed as if she might press clothes or take in sewing, detached herself from the crowd where she had been standing near the Putnam brothers. Slow but not halting, she marched to the hotel, went in, and came out a couple of minutes later.

She had with her a young woman in her twenties, not

anything glamorous but not homely, either. The girl was wearing a dark blue wool cap that matched her jacket and long skirt. She had a light complexion, brown curls beneath her cap, and light-colored eyes. She walked with the woman named Blanche and stepped up onto the platform as Blanche stood by on the ground.

"Thank you," said Bill. Turning to the girl, he said, "Thank you for coming today. Would you please tell us your name?"

"Rhoda Walsh." She pursed her red lips when she finished.

"And can you tell us why you came?"

"Because you asked me to. And you paid my way. I couldn't have come on my own."

"Your time in itself is valuable. Now, can you tell us the purpose in your coming here?"

"Well, it's like you said. To tell who gave me the necklace."

"This one?"

Bill held out his hand at chest level, and a polished medallion the size of a five-dollar gold piece swung on a thin gold chain. As the shiny object moved, a red stone sparkled in the sunlight.

"Yes, that's it."

"And can you tell us who gave it to you?"

"A man named Ned Putnam." She kept from looking at the crowd. "He was courting me in Laramie, but in the end, I turned him down. I would prefer not to say why."

Vic Putnam's voice burst out. "Now see here! I don't know what you think you're going to prove, but I can't stand by and watch you drag a man's reputation through the mud. He went through a big disappointment, and that should be enough."

Eyes turned to Ned, who raised his chin and put on a somber expression.

Bill's voice was steady, and I thought he must have prepared his words. "He was in possession of a piece of jewelry that was taken from a murdered woman."

Vic waved his hand. "That's what you say."

"He can hardly deny that he was in possession of it. As for where it came from, you don't have to take my word for it. I have someone else who can identify it."

Vic sniffed and rubbed his mustache. "It's hard to believe someone who's been to jail."

"I haven't lied about a thing. And the person I speak of is here among us."

A hush settled on the crowd as the people looked at those around them. From the opposite edge of the crowd, a man in a short-brimmed hat and dark traveling suit stepped forward and mounted the platform. I could see right away that he had a brown complexion, and from his features I thought he might be part Negro. He stood at the left edge of the stage, while Rhoda Walsh, pale with red lipstick, stood at the right.

"My thanks to you for coming," said Bill. "To move things along, could you tell us your name?"

In a plain, clear voice, the man said, "Eugene Hughes."

"And what relation do you have to the case?"

"My sister was the person who owned that piece of jewelry. Her name was Ellie Hughes."

Bill held the pendant toward the man. "This one."

Eugene stepped forward and let the medallion lie in his fingers. "Yes, that's it. With the same inscription."

Rhoda Walsh had covered her mouth as she gasped and stepped back to the edge of the stage.

Bill turned to her. "Is there something—?"

Rhoda stammered, "Wa-was she—?"

A voice from the front row called out, "A mulatto."

Eugene turned to the man and said, "We are Creole."

Silence hung for a moment. I did not know how anyone around me felt, but it was impressive for me to hear a colored person speak up for himself.

Morg Salter spoke in a slow and deliberate way, after having been quiet for a few minutes. "So you mean to say, that this isn't just a case of possession of stolen property." It seemed to be sinking into him as he said it.

"That's right," said Bill. "No one has even thought to say that he bought it in a pawn shop. And it's not just the case of a common thief stealing a ring to put on a girl's finger. It's a crime of force. Put it together. You've worked for them since the Sybille Ditch project. You remember the towns you went to."

Salter's eyes tightened as he peered at his two bosses. Muttering traveled through the crowd, and I heard the words "law," "sheriff," "lock 'em up."

Vic Putnam moved away from those around him, and his eyes met those of his brother. Quick on his feet, Vic took hold of the woman named Blanche and put the barrel of his pistol against her cheekbone. "No one's goin' to do anything," he said.

Ned followed suit, springing onto the stage and laying his hand on Rhoda Walsh's upper arm.

She had an expression of contempt as she jerked her elbow backward, twisted away, and said, "Don't put your hands on me."

Bill had his gun drawn and said, "Hold it right there, both of you. Let the women go."

With Rhoda out of the way, Ned fired. A red spot appeared on Bill's buckskin shirt, but Bill put two bullets into Ned's chest and knocked him over backward.

Blanche, meanwhile, was squirming enough to break loose, and she stumbled and fell to the ground. Vic brought his six-gun around to point it at Bill, and the two of them fired at the same time. A second red spot appeared on Bill's shirt, and he fell flat on his rump with his legs spread out. Vic Putnam took one step backward and spilled over on his side.

Most of the people in the crowd had pushed way back, and some of them had run away. Eugene Hughes came forward from where he had gotten out of the line of fire. He knelt by Bill and held him up.

I moved to see Bill's face, and he smiled at me. "Come here," he said.

My legs felt unsteady as I stepped up onto the platform and drew close. I knelt along with Eugene.

Bill said, "I didn't want it to come to this. I wanted to expose them and then have them face the law. I should have planned it better. I put too much stake in making it public."

Eugene said, "I think you got yourself shot pretty bad."

"Oh, I did. I can tell." Bill raised his left hand, where the thin gold chain was twined in his finger. He handed the medallion to Eugene and said, "I want you to have this."

Eugene took the chain and medallion. "She would appreciate what you did."

Bill let out a sigh. "Maybe so. But I never felt good enough for her."

"Don't worry about that now."

"I suppose not. I don't have long." With his other hand, Bill raised his pistol.

I drew back because it was pointed at me.

He said, "No, no, kid. I want to give this to you. This and the holster."

"I don't—"

"I want you to have it. It's all I've got except for my horse and saddle. I want Garry the kitchen boy to have them."

"Are you sure?" said Eugene.

"Yes, I am. You both heard me."

"Anything else?"

Bill shook his head. His eyes were going dull. "No, just let me lie down."

"What about your ring?"

"I'd like to keep it."

In another minute, he was gone. My throat was swelled up, and I had nothing to say. I fought against the tears that came to my eyes.

A voice spoke from above my shoulder. I recognized it as Morg Salter's. "You can never be sure how well you know someone."

I understood him to mean the Putnam brothers.

He sniffed and went on. "Even this fella here. He wasn't as bad as I thought."

I stood up and swallowed hard. I could not make myself speak. I could not say how sorry I was that Bill died for taking all the trouble he did to bring out the truth, and I could not say, though I believed it, that he was good enough.

★ ★ ★ ★ ★

Next to the Last Chance

★ ★ ★ ★ ★

I

For the last mile into the ranch, a cold, light rain had given way to thin snow. Dunn tied his horse to the rail outside the stable and made short work of pulling off the saddle and blankets and storing them inside. He led the bay into the corral, turned the animal around, and slipped off the bridle. The dark horse stood for a second, held by the bond between horse and rider, and turned away. Dunn closed the gate behind him on his way to the stable, where he hung the bridle on a peg.

He crossed the yard at a brisk pace, passing the abandoned ranch house with its gaunt windows and the pyramid-shaped roof falling in. Light showed in the window of the bunkhouse, and smoke was rising and spilling out of the stovepipe. Dunn made for the door, laid his hand on the cold, wet doorknob, and pushed his way inside. Warm air met him, mixed with lamplight and wisps of smoke. A fire crackled in the sheet-metal stove, and a spark flew out through the open door.

Dunn blinked and found Percy, bareheaded with his sleeves rolled up, slicing potatoes on a cutting board.

"Made it back," said the boss.

"None too soon." Dunn shook his upper body and shrugged out of his canvas coat. He draped it on the back of a chair near the fire, then took off his hat and swept it back and forth to shake off the loose moisture.

"Get the fence fixed all right?"

"I suppose." Dunn held his palms to the stove and recalled

167

the slipshod repairs he had had to make, splicing and re-splicing rusty wire and using bent nails for staples. "Whoever put in that fence must not have had good wire."

"That was in the early days. Bob wire was new."

"It's a nuisance to have to put one patch onto another."

"Wal, you know, big outfits can afford to put in a new fence. I can only do so much."

"Yeah." Dunn rotated his hands against the warmth. He recognized the boss's theme, how the big outfits could do as they please, manage the rules of the range to their advantage, and have money for men and equipment. The little man, as Percy McFarland called himself, had to do what he could to get by. He had to look out for himself, and keeping a man to maverick a few head in the off-season was one way to do it. Having that same man mend fences put a good face on things.

"Got some grub on the way." Percy spoke in a rising tone, as was his habit when he changed the topic. "Some spuds an' onions, and it always tastes better when it's someone else's beef."

"I'll get cleaned up."

"Sure. I didn't think to put a basin of water on the stove, but there's time if you want to."

"I'm not that cold. But it's chilly and damp out there, and I had to work with my bare hands most of the time, to deal with all the twisted wire. Then it seems like all I have to do is get close to barbed wire, and I cut myself."

"Isn't that the truth." Percy set a skillet on the stove top and spooned in some bacon grease.

The mixture of grub was sputtering in the cast-iron pan when Dunn took a chair near the stove. The boss stood nearby, flapper in hand, gazing at the stove top.

Dunn gave the man credit for being deeper than he let on. Percy had a simple appearance, being of middle height with a bald head, suspenders, and a working man's forearms. Eating someone else's beef was a matter of good humor in cow country, as almost everyone did it, with the understanding that it all evened out. But Dunn had helped Percy deliver a steer here and a heifer there, to work camps where no bill of sale was recorded and where the hide and brand disappeared. All the while, Percy presented himself as the little man who couldn't afford new lumber or a spool of barbed wire.

"Workin' on another idea," said Percy, not quite in his light, cheery tone.

"You mean work?" Dunn did not know Percy to joke about whiskey or women, though he did not seem to be the kind to turn down either one if it did not cost him much.

"That's right. Get away from fence-fixin' for a little while." The boss poked at the food and moved it around in the skillet. "There's another small operation, fellas I met, and I made an agreement to work with them. See how it works out."

Dunn inhaled. The aroma of fried meat, potatoes, and onions gave a pleasant effect, a promise of satisfaction. "What's their name?"

"The outfit doesn't have a name. Just fellas that work together. They've set up a cow camp down at the old Pickerall Station."

Dunn nodded as he placed it, several miles south of the ranch and a little west.

"I'd like to send you over there. You'd still be workin' for me, but you'd do as they tell you. Take your bag and bedroll. They should have everything for a camp."

"Ride my own horse?"

"That should be all right to begin with."

Dunn saddled the dark horse beneath a grey morning sky. The snow had let up, but the sunlight did not break through the stark cover, and a chilly wind blew in light, intermittent breaths from the northwest. The horse stood still as Dunn tied on his rifle and scabbard, bedroll, and duffel bag. As a matter of course, he rode his own horse every three or four days and the boss's stock the rest of the time, so the animal was rested but not too fresh. Dunn walked the horse out a half dozen steps, checked the cinch, and swung aboard.

With an early start and with no direct instructions on how soon to arrive at the cow camp, Dunn turned his horse southeast. With his back to the wind, he headed toward town.

Snow lay in tiny drifts along the edges of the main street of Brigstock. A couple of horses were tied to hitching rails, and a ranch wagon stood in front of the mercantile. Farther down the street on the left, the area in front of the Hillrose Café was bare, which suited Dunn all right. He rode that far, dismounted, tied up in front, and walked in.

The tables on both sides were empty, and no one stood behind the counter at the back. Dunn imagined that the bell on the door would bring someone, and he felt a flush of pleasure at the sight of a blond head of hair and a white apron. Milly let the kitchen door swing closed behind her as she walked to the end of the counter.

She turned, tipped her head, and said, "Hello, stranger."

"Top of the morning to you." He sauntered to the end of the counter, set his hat on the surface, and moved to meet her.

He put his arms around her waist, and she turned away to let him kiss her cheek. Her hair, the color of sun-bleached wheat stubble, was pinned up in tight waves, and the scent of bath powder stirred him. He moved his hand up to the bottom of her breast, and she took it away.

He made a playful pout as they turned to face each other.

She tipped her head again, in a mixture of teasing and scolding. "I already told you. That's for later."

He pursed his lips. There had already been one time, on a sunny day, when it was not for later. He had told her since then that he would like to take her back to Glover Canyon, and she had told him in response that they weren't doing it again until later, so he saw no point in saying anything more at the moment. But he had a full sense of her presence, swathed though it was in a full grey dress and a white apron.

"What's new?" She lifted her head in a glance toward the street, where his horse stood.

"Percy's sending me on a job, with some other fellows who are at a place southwest of here. What used to be the old Pickerall Station. Supposed to be a cow camp."

"No names?"

"The outfit doesn't have a name, and he didn't give me any names for the men at this point."

"Well, I hope there's some money in it for you."

"Same as always. I'm still working for Percy, and he's kind of a skinflint."

"That's how people end up with money. They let others have as little as possible."

"Maybe it works for him."

"George, too." Milly rolled her eyes toward the kitchen.

"Can he hear you?"

"He's not here right now."

"Must be taking all his money to the bank."

"Could be. How long are you going to be gone?"

"I don't know. A few days at least. Depends on how much work they have. Or what kind it is."

Milly let out a tired breath. "I wish you could make some money so we could go somewhere."

"So do I. A change would do me some good as well."

She flicked her eyebrows. "I'd like to go someplace where I

don't have to smile and pour coffee for every Romeo with two bits."

Movement outside caught Dunn's eye, but it was just his horse shifting its position with the weight on its back. "I don't care so much about where I go or what kind of work I do, within reason, of course, but I'd like to feel better about how I spend my life."

"That's pretty close to the same thing."

"It might be. I'm not sure. Maybe I could have said it clearer."

"Oh, no. I understand you."

He laughed to himself. Maybe that was why he didn't get what he wanted. He was too easy to understand.

The cloud cover did not lift, and Dunn had the chill wind on the side of his face as he headed toward Pickerall Station. He did not have a clear idea of what kind of work to expect. Most if not all outfits would have shipped their beef cattle by how. With fall roundup over, they would have turned their cattle and common workhorses onto the range for the winter and would have paid off the hands who worked for the season.

Some men broke and trained horses in the winter. Others did indoor work, like mending harnesses and repairing wagons. Still others trapped or hunted or cut firewood. If Dunn was going to a work camp, he might be put to doing camp work, and he might be expected to bring in meat or wood. Then there was other work that he preferred not to imagine in detail right now, work he had done in off-seasons in the past, when stock animals came and went and a man moved around as he needed. Dunn admitted to himself that he had not yet decided when would be the last time he would do that kind of work.

Dry weeds stuck up around the front steps of the two shacks at Pickerall Station, and sparse growth showed in the bare ground where the corrals had once stood. Dunn had ridden past the station a couple of times, and he had never seen signs of human activity. He knew it had been a way station on an old freight line, and the box canyon in back had served as a pasture for draft animals. He imagined that a small spring flowed a ways back in on the left, where chokecherry bushes and a few scrubby box elder trees now stood leafless.

Dunn brought his horse to a stop and called out. A few seconds later, he called again. The two weathered buildings remained silent as the wind whispered around them. Dunn was about to turn away when the door of the shack on the right scuffed open.

A man appeared, bareheaded and in stocking feet, squinting at the dull light. He rubbed his face and said, "Yeah?"

"Percy McFarland sent me down this way to lend a hand."

"Yeah, yeah. Wait a minute. I'll be right out." The man stepped back and closed the door.

Dunn dismounted and used his horse for a windbreak as he rolled a cigarette and lit it. The wind blew, unsteady. Dunn thought he heard a voice inside the shack, but the sound was brief and muffled. It could have been a chair scraping.

Dunn had smoked his cigarette down and pinched out the snipe when the door opened again. The man with the flushed face stepped outside, now wearing a dark, dusty hat, a coat of dull black sackcloth that reached to his knees, and stovepipe boots with denim trousers tucked in. A gunbelt showed when the coat moved.

"Now who are you again?"

"My name's Joe Dunn. I work for Percy McFarland."

"Oh, yeah. Jug said he would send someone."

Dunn tossed a glance at the shack. He guessed Jug was the boss. "Is your foreman here?"

"No. Just me and Rod. He'll be here later."

"And you are—?"

"Art." The man did not offer to shake. "You might as well unload your stuff. Put it in here with us. The other one's the cookhouse. Jug'll stay there."

"Do the saddles go inside, too?"

"Unless you want to leave it out in the rain."

"I didn't know if there was a stable or a lean-to in back."

"There isn't."

Dunn tied his horse to a hitching rail between the two shacks and took down his bag, bedroll, and rifle scabbard. He carried them to the front door, which stood ajar, and pushed it open as he knocked on it.

The surly man's voice sounded. "Come on in."

Dunn stepped into the one-room shack, a dark area with the stale odors of old cigarette smoke and the breaths of people who slept in a confined space. Daylight straggling in through the doorway showed beds, saddles, and personal belongings strewn all over the floor. The man called Art sat in a chair, as if he was resting from his recent exertion, and a second man lay in a bed on the floor with a pair of boots and a pistol close at hand.

Art cleared his throat with a short cough. "You can find room against the wall there."

Dunn set his gear on the floor. "Where should I put my horse?"

"There's a pasture in back. You'll find it."

Dunn left his saddle and blankets on the hitching rail and led his horse around back. Fifty yards behind the buildings, a three-wire fence stretched across the mouth of the canyon. Dunn led the horse in through the wire gate, turned him, and took off the bridle. Dunn stood with his back to the gate as usual, patted the horse on the neck, and dismissed him.

"Good boy."

The dark horse turned and wandered off to see what the pasture held.

The second man was sitting up in his bed smoking a cigarette when Dunn carried his saddle and blankets into the shack and set them with his other gear. Daylight through the open door showed a man with thinning hair and a light-colored mustache that grew down past the corners of his mouth. He turned to the side, blew out a puff of smoke, and directed his attention upward to Dunn.

"How-do?"

"Mornin'. My name's Joe Dunn. Percy sent me."

"That's what Art said. I'm Rod Hunter."

"Is that open door giving you a draft?"

"Nah. A little fresh air doesn't hurt, and the light helps. We're goin' to go over to the cookshack in a little while." Hunter raised his head and pulled on the back of his neck with his cupped hand. "Son of a bitch."

"Rough night?"

"I've seen worse. Leave it to Stanberry to bring such rotten whiskey."

The other man spoke up. "I bought what they had. Next time, you can do it."

Dunn figured that some of this light bickering was for his benefit. "I'll wait outside," he said.

Stanberry and Hunter emerged from the shack in a little while, and Dunn followed them into the other building, which was the larger of the two. It was a two-room affair, with a cast-iron stove in the front room that must have been left behind because of its weight. The table and two benches, made of rough lumber with split ends and showing a few bent-over nails, might have been brought in after the way station occupants left. The other piece of furniture was a stump, cut even across the top and bottom, which would serve as a seat or a work area. The room in back, as Dunn could see through the open door, was empty, but he could imagine it turning into a boar's nest like the place next door.

Percy had said these fellows would have everything for a camp, but Dunn didn't see much—a smudged coffeepot, a skillet, a few tin plates and utensils, a small burlap bag with maybe a dozen potatoes, and a side of bacon wrapped in brown paper with grease spots.

Hunter pulled on the back of his neck and rolled his head. "Get a fire goin' in the son of a bitch."

Stanberry said, "We're gonna need more wood."

Dunn recognized one of the jobs he had imagined for himself. "I'll go look for some."

Back in the canyon a ways, he found a couple of dead branches that earlier wood-gatherers must have left behind. The thickest parts were about an inch and a half across, which seemed not so bad to Dunn, as he had not seen an ax or hatchet anywhere in the camp. He dragged the two branches to the cookshack, and with a pair of leather gloves, he broke up the wood into stove lengths until he came to thicker widths. He stepped and jumped on the last few pieces, and in the end, he had a small stack that might cook one meal.

He joined Stanberry and Hunter for a midday meal of fried potatoes and boiled coffee. He did not ask questions, but from the conversation, some of which he thought, again, was for his benefit, he derived that Jug, their leader, would be here later in the day with plans to move a few head of stock.

Dunn began to have a clearer idea of what kind of a cow camp this was. In a lighter moment, at some distance, he would call it a robbers' roost. He recognized that at some point he would have to give up this kind of work, as there was no good future in hanging out with criminals and doing their work. At one moment and another, he observed Stanberry and Hunter, eating fried potatoes and drinking black coffee just as he was doing. He did not see them as his people; he saw them as strangers. At the same time, he recognized that he was like them in a way he had not admitted to himself until now.

The grey sky did not appear to change as Dunn made a couple of more trips into the canyon for dead branches. The exercise served to keep him warm as well as to help pass the time. The dark horse kept him company, nipping on his sleeve and playing with his gloves when he left them on the ground.

He broke up the wood into pieces and added to the stack he had begun earlier. None of it would last long. The thinner pieces would burn in an instant, and even the pieces he had to break with his feet would burn out in ten minutes or so. At least he was doing something useful, and the work helped him feel different from his two new associates.

He moved all the fuel inside, where the previous pile had dwindled to a few sticks. The new supply gave him a moment of satisfaction, but he imagined it would go up in flame and smoke that evening.

At the moment, the cookhouse had a cold and gloomy atmosphere. Stanberry and Hunter had retired to the other shack, and the fire from midday had long since burned out. Dunn put on his coat and went outside to sit on the front step.

He rolled a cigarette and lit it. As he blew out the smoke, he let his gaze wander out across the rangeland. Nothing moved amidst the dull tones of sagebrush and dry grass. He figured the time at about four o'clock. Daylight would begin to fade pretty soon. At this time of year, this far north, the sun went down early whether a person could see it or not.

When he finished the cigarette, he pushed himself up and went inside for his gloves, which he had left on the table. His body heat had subsided as he sat in the cooling air, and his

177

hands had stiffened after all the work of breaking up branches. He put on his gloves, waved his arms back and forth, and stepped outside again where the light was still better.

His pulse jumped at the sight of two riders, dark figures against the landscape. He walked the short distance to the other shack, knocked on the door, and pushed it open.

Stanberry and Hunter were sitting in the two available chairs, each with an elbow on a small table that Dunn had not noticed earlier. They were smoking cigarettes, and a stub of a candle between them gave a bit of light.

"Two riders coming," said Dunn.

Stanberry yawned. "Must be Jug. I hope he brought something."

Hunter stretched out his arms and stood up. "We'll see."

Dunn left them and made his way outside. The two riders were closer now, and he could see that they had different shapes. The one on the left might be a woman.

Footsteps sounded as Stanberry and Hunter came up on Dunn's left. Hunter said, "It's Jug, all right."

No one spoke further as the two riders clip-clopped in on their hard-breathing horses and passed in front of the three men standing. Packs and bundles were tied onto the saddles, and both riders wore dark drover coats.

The man swung down, tied his horse at the rail, and came around in a visible swagger. He let the woman dismount by herself, which she did by pulling her right knee up to her chin, dragging her boot across the cantle, dislodging her left foot from the stirrup as she clutched the saddle horn with both hands, and sliding down the side of the saddle.

Dunn made himself not look at her. He kept his eyes on the man, who drew himself up in front of the others. He wore a flat-brimmed, flat-crowned hat, dark brown, and had light brown hair that grew over his ears and down to his collar. He had a full beard, darker than his hair, and a few broken blood vessels showed on his face. His plain brown eyes moved from side to side and settled on Dunn.

"I'm Jug."

"I'm Joe Dunn."

"McFarland said you should be here."

Stanberry spoke up. "Did you bring more grub?"

"I said I would. You'll see for yourself when you unpack my horse. Rod, you can help with the stuff on Verna's horse." Jug took in a full breath, exhaled through his nose, and said, "Dunn, you can take care of the horses."

Jug stood back, squared his shoulders, and took out the makings for a cigarette. He pulled in a long sniff through one nostril and went to work rolling a cigarette. When he lit it, he walked around to the back of the cookshack.

Dunn stood out of the way as the other two men untied the lashes on the horses. The woman waited until Hunter swung down a brown leather gripsack and handed it to her.

She hefted it and walked free of the horses. Dunn thought she would turn without looking at him and trudge right into the shack, but she paused and let her eyes meet his.

"Good afternoon. I'm Verna."

"And good afternoon to you. My name is Joe Dunn." He took the instant to appreciate her dark hair, tanned face, and hazel eyes. He knew she was keeping track of Jug, or she wouldn't have given Dunn more than a glance. He took off his hat and said, "Pleased to meet you."

"The same here." She gave a faint smile and a nod, swung the grip into motion, and headed into the building.

Dunn helped with the untying and kept track of the lash cords and ropes, which he put into one canvas saddlebag. He did not presume to touch anything that looked like someone's personal effects, and he did not carry anything into the shack until he stripped the horses of their saddles and blankets. When he had the horses put away in the pasture, he took the two bridles into what was now the main building.

Two tall candles with one-inch flames were producing good light. Cigarette smoke hung in the air, and warmth spread from the stove. Jug sat on one side of the table with his two underlings across from him. A bottle of whiskey sat on the table between them.

Verna crouched at the stump with her back to the men, moving her arm as a knife blade clacked on a cutting board. A skillet was starting to sizzle, and Dunn caught the first whiff of frying bacon.

"Have a seat," said Jug.

Dunn gave his attention to the men. The only space was on the bench next to Jug. When Dunn sat down, he saw that he would have to turn his head to see Verna, and he thought that was for the best.

Jug said, "It looks like we're goin' to be here for a couple of days or more. Just waiting. We brought some grub, but it's not goin' to last that long." He tipped his ash in a sardine can and turned his head toward Dunn. "I'm goin' to send you to town for supplies. Tomorrow. I don't want you to waste any time."

"I don't."

"McFarland says you're sweet on a biscuit shooter. You don't need to be telling her what you know."

"I don't know anything." Dunn waited for Jug's next comment, but the man remained silent. Dunn had a sense of Verna's presence and could hear the scraping of a skillet on the stove top. He wondered if any of Jug's remarks were for Verna's benefit or if, along with his silence, they were just part of his general purpose of showing who was cock of the roost.

II

The dark horse stood still and let Dunn put the halter on him. Out of habit, Dunn counted the other horses in the pasture. He found all four in a moment. In no hurry, he reviewed them. The sorrel with no markings and the light-built bay had been in the pasture when Dunn arrived the day before, so they belonged to, or at least pertained to, Stanberry and Hunter. The stocky brown horse was the one that Jug had ridden into camp, and the light-colored one with a black mane and tail, which people called a grey horse, had carried Verna.

Dunn scanned the four again. The men all had mounts suitable for night work, as he himself did. Horses with white markings, such as a blaze, matched socks, or a splash on the hip, made for good photographs, along with cowboys in nice duds. More than once on a roundup crew, Dunn had seen a number of men turn out on white horses for a picture. But men who threw the long rope kept to dark clothes and dark horses—as did the men who tracked and hunted them. Dunn shook off the last thought and led his horse to the gate.

Town at midmorning had about the same activity as the day before. As he had not been instructed not to visit at the café, and as he felt a small resentment toward Jug's sarcastic comments, Dunn stopped at the Hillrose Café and tied his horse.

Two men in coats and winter caps were coming out as Dunn went in. Milly stood behind the counter at the back of the business, calm and observing. She did not move around to the end of the counter, and Dunn wondered if George, the boss, was in the kitchen.

Milly tapped a pencil on the back of her hand, then set the pencil down. "Good day to you. Back in town again already."

He came to a stop a couple of yards from the counter. "Seems like just yesterday."

"Doesn't it, though? What's new in the world?"

"Not much. Just came in for provisions. Thought I'd stop here first."

"For the camp at the way station?"

"Something like that."

"What kind of cattle are you working?"

"None yet."

"Everyone has to eat, though."

"That's true."

She smiled and brought her blue eyes to meet his. "Any names yet?"

"Eeny, Meeny, and Miny."

She gave a light frown and tipped her head. "Are we playing blindman's buff?"

"Only if we play the version where the blindfolded person gets kissed."

"Any idea of how long you'll be there?"

"None so far. Nothing specific, anyway. A few days, at least."

"I heard it snowed up north."

"How far north?"

"Four Corners."

"That's a long ways."

"Is Percy making money on this deal?"

"I imagine he hopes to make money off of any piece of business. But nobody tells me anything."

"I know the feeling."

"Look, honey, I'll tell you what I can, when I can. Sometimes it's better not to know anything."

"You do a good job of that."

Dunn was going to tell her he worked hard at it, but the doorbell tinkled, and he saw her boss coming through the front door. "I'll be going," he said.

"Come again."

Dunn imagined she said that to all the customers and that she was saying it loud enough for George to hear. Dunn nodded to the proprietor on the way out. George carried the newspaper in one hand and four cigars in the other. He nodded to Dunn as if to acknowledge that his had been only a social visit.

Verna was waiting for groceries when Dunn returned to the camp, and she began unpacking them right away. Jug was sitting at the table. He took out a pocketknife and began to clean his nails as Dunn brought in the rest of the packages and set them on the table. As Verna started a fire in the stove, Dunn asked if there was anything else he should do before he put his horse away.

Jug said, "Not right now. But after dinner, you could go out and scare up some more firewood. The boys said you know where to find it."

"Where anyone would know to look. It would help if I had an ax, though. All I brought in yesterday was stuff I could break by hand."

"Wondered about that. You should have asked. The boys had one."

"I didn't see it."

"That's not the same as there not bein' one."

"I guess I'll put my horse away, then."

Jug did not answer.

Verna nodded but did not look straight at Dunn.

Stanberry and Hunter were sitting in the two chairs when Dunn put his saddle and blankets in the shack. Dunn had left his rifle and scabbard on the floor near his bed, and he was glad to see them in the same place. Returning to the center of the room, he spoke to the others.

"Jug said there was an ax around here somewhere. I'd like to use it after dinner."

Hunter stood up. He was wearing his hat and boots and gun-belt. He drew himself up to his full height and strode across the room. After a pause, he leaned over and rummaged in a pile of tarpaulins and ropes, and he brought out a single-bit ax with a flat head. He strolled back to the spot where Dunn stood, and he set the ax head-down on the floor and held the handle erect with his finger on the tip.

"Here's one."

"Thanks."

"It was here yesterday."

"I didn't see it."

"I guess not."

Hunter released the handle, and Dunn caught it before it could fall. Hunter rolled his shoulders as he walked back toward his chair.

Dunn frowned. He wondered what to make of Hunter's demeanor. He recalled that both men seemed a bit puffed up the evening before, and he attributed their manner to the whiskey. Now he wondered if it was the presence of the woman as well. Hunter had been working nearby when Verna stopped to introduce herself to Dunn. Maybe he harbored some resentment or jealousy. Maybe it was simpler. From his exchange with Jug, Dunn had formed the impression that the other three had talked about him while he went to town, and they might have shared an unspoken assumption that he was the lowest one in the pecking order.

Stanberry rose halfway from his seat, and with a downward thrust, he stuck a straight-handled knife in the wood floor. When the knife quivered to a stop, Dunn saw that the handle was made of a ruby-colored, glass-like material and had the shape of a woman's naked body.

Stanberry's voice sounded gravelly as he said, "What do you think of that?"

Dunn had seen a letter knife and a bottle opener with handles like the one on Stanberry's knife, although his was larger, as it was part of a stiletto with a six-inch blade. He had also seen objects of a similar nature—the shank of a boot spur in the form of a woman's leg, and a bootjack or boot puller in the shape of a woman's open legs.

"I've seen the style before, in wood and in ivory or something like it. Then similar things cast in metal."

Stanberry leaned over and pulled the knife out of the floorboard. "It fits the hand. You can put your thumb on her boobies and your finger on her rump. She can't take it away from you. Ha-ha." He poked the blade into a sheath of thin leather. "See? You keep her where you want her. Not like some women. They have all the control. They give it to you, and then they take it away, and they've got you eatin' out of their hand, 'cause you're hopin' they'll let you have it again."

Dunn felt a pained expression take over his face, and he made an effort to clear it. He wondered if Stanberry had any way of knowing . . . no, he couldn't. Uncanny though it was, Dunn was sure it was just the regular talk of a man of that kind.

Stanberry polished the handle with his thumb. " 'Some certain snatch.' That's Shakespeare. I bet you didn't know that."

Dunn said, "All I've read is *Romeo and Juliet.*"

Stanberry shrugged. "I don't know which one it's from."

"You could look it up someday," said Hunter. "When you have a lot of time on your hands."

"I don't plan to."

"No one does."

Dunn thought this was just more banter, but whether it was about women or prison, it came from somewhere.

★ ★ ★ ★ ★

Dunn had finished his breakfast of hotcakes and molasses and was sipping a cup of coffee when Jug spoke.

"Dunn, I'm goin' to send you out to look around. I want you to ride about halfway to McFarland's and then come back on a half-circle to here. Curl around toward town but don't go in there. See what you see. Keep out of sight to the extent that you can."

"And if anyone asks me what I'm doing?"

"You're workin' for McFarland." Jug shifted the tone of his voice as he spoke to Stanberry and Hunter. "You two, do the other half of a circle, but in reverse order. Curve around to the west, and when you get to the far point north, come straight back here."

Stanberry said, "Like yesterday."

"Yes, but you go north, not south."

"Yeah, yeah."

Stanberry and Hunter had taken their horses out the afternoon before when Dunn was gathering wood, but they did not say where they were going, and he did not ask. As he pictured this morning's work, he realized that either or both of them would be at his back at some point, and he wondered if Jug let him know that much so that he would have the sense not to slip into town.

He was not tempted to stray, anyway. He caught his horse, saddled up, and rode north. He felt free under the wide, grey sky, and although he was keeping an eye out to see which cattle were where, he had the satisfaction of being able to say, if only to himself, that he was minding his own business.

His ride blended into a quiet, almost muted atmosphere. He did not miss the whining gnats and buzzing flies of summer, or even the clacking grasshoppers, but the rangeland seemed somber without the tinkling tune of the meadowlark. The

186

antelope formed large herds and kept their distance at this time of year, as he recalled when he saw a tribe of about thirty, streaking away to the east in silence.

Cattle were few, but he noted the brands. He did not see any unbranded stock, nor did he see any loose horses. This part of the range had been grazed close and would not support more than a few head per section, so he was not surprised to see so little livestock.

The dark horse spooked when a jackrabbit sprang up from a clump of sagebrush and bolted away on its zigzag route. The horse settled down, and Dunn went on his uneventful way.

When he estimated that he was at the midpoint between the camp and McFarland's ranch, he began to curve around to the east. He imagined his semicircle to be like the face of the clock. He would be closest to town at the three, and then he would move farther away.

Although the sun did not show, he had a fair sense of direction. He practiced keeping out of sight, not skylining himself or barging into plain view. By practicing his plainscraft, he made a successful sneak, without trying, upon a gang of nine antelope. This time he heard their huffing and the rustling of their hooves as they bolted away. One of them had a high set of black horns, and he moved in the middle of the pack as the group raced over the next rise and disappeared.

Dunn was between the one and the two on his imagined path when an object in the distance caused him to stop his horse and slip down from the saddle. He led the horse to lower ground and followed the contour of the land. The rider was headed toward town, and Dunn wanted to get a look at him.

Keeping the horse back as far as his arm and the reins would allow, Dunn took slow steps toward the crest. The rider came into view again, less than a quarter of a mile away. The sorrel horse with two white socks was moving at a fast walk, and the rider sat straight and sturdy in the saddle. Dunn recognized the horse and the rider. Although a low-crowned hat kept the bald head out of view, Dunn knew his boss, Percy McFarland.

Dunn sank back and let out a long breath. After all of his stealth, he saw the one person he did not have to hide from. Still, he was doing his job, and he now had something to report.

Jug did not look up from rolling a cigarette as Dunn told him what he had seen.

"He's got a right to come and go as he pleases, and he doesn't need to keep us informed, but it's all interesting. Maybe he's got a puss in town."

Verna was whacking a spoon on the lip of a pot of beans, and she did not show any indication of having heard. Dunn was glad that Stanberry and Hunter had not come in yet.

"What else did you see?"

"A mix of cattle. Cows, calves, yearling heifers, and steers. Nothing unbranded. Mostly two or three brands from around here."

"Two, or three?"

"Well, three. Now that I think of it, I didn't see any bulls."

"There's some out there, no doubt of that. But we don't care about them, anyway."

"What do we care about?"

"Just what you saw."

"Then that's it. Plus a few antelope and jackrabbits."

Jug held the cigarette in the side of his mouth as he struck a match and lit his smoke. After he shook out the match, he opened and closed his right hand a couple of times. "Sometimes this son of a bitch gets stiff on me. I wonder if it means there's a storm coming."

Verna had cleared the table and was washing the noon dishes

with her back to the men. Their seating arrangement remained the same, with Jug on Dunn's left, Hunter across from Dunn, and Stanberry across from Jug. All four were smoking cigarettes, and the front door was open.

Stanberry was talking about snakes, how he had not seen one for over a month, and this was the time of year when they denned up. Like bears.

"Don't kid yourself about bears," said Hunter. "I've seen black bears in the mountains when there was a foot of snow on the ground. They'll run from a man. But a grizzly won't. You meet one of them this time of year, when they're puttin' on the feed, and you won't have as much of a chance as a one-legged Indian in an ass-kickin' contest."

Stanberry said, "I've never been in one of those. How do you win?"

"Pick your opponent," said Jug.

Stanberry didn't let up. "Ha-ha. But some of 'em will have two legs. I was going to say, if you're inside, keep your back to the wall."

Jug sniffed. "That's an old joke from somewhere else."

Hunter said, "When we were kids, we used to have one-legged fights. Hold up one foot with your hand and hop on the other, and try to knock down the others by bumpin' into 'em."

Stanberry's voice took on its gravelly tone. "We did that, too. Also leg-wrestled and arm-wrestled."

Hunter sat up straight and took in a breath. "Now arm wrestling, that's something I still do."

"Yeah, yeah," said Stanberry.

"Jug doesn't care for it."

"Not because I couldn't beat you, but because I'm not going to ruin my arm. I know a fellow who did, and he couldn't throw a rock after that."

"I beat Art, and he can still throw a rock."

189

Jug did not answer.

Hunter faced Dunn. "How about you? We're about the same size, same age. It's not as if I'd be picking on an old man."

Dunn tried to ignore the sarcasm. He had placed all three of the men as being in the same age range as he was, the mid-thirties. He had a sense of Verna being present, and he was sure that Hunter did, too. "I don't care to compete," he said.

"You mean you don't want to lose."

"That's not what I said."

"This is a good place for it. No one has the back of a chair to brace himself. The way I do it, both men keep their free hand on the table, and they hook onto one another with their little fingers. Keep your elbow between your thumb and first finger, like this." Hunter had his left hand flat and his right elbow in the notch, with his forearm upright.

"I can see how it's done, but I don't want to."

"I don't blame you. I wouldn't want to lose, either."

Jug said, "Do you play baseball? They have to throw straight."

"No, I don't," said Dunn.

"Neither do I. There's no money in it."

Breakfast consisted of hotcakes and molasses again. As he ate, Dunn reviewed the sameness of the past few days. For three afternoons in a row, he had gathered firewood. For two meals the day before, they had eaten biscuits and beans. Now they were having hotcakes a second time. Dunn was not picky about what he ate, and he was used to routine, but he thought something should have happened by now.

With the exception of the one occasion when Jug told him what he would do the next day, Jug did not tell him what to do until it was time. That pattern had also become evident, so Dunn drank his coffee and kept to his own thoughts.

As Verna was taking away Jug's plate, the boss turned to

Dunn and said, "I'm going to send you up to McFarland's with a message. He'll see that he needs to send a message back."

"What if he's not there?"

"Then you wait until he is. I need to hear back from him."

"All right."

"If he's not there, don't go to town lookin' for him. Wait until he comes back."

"I understand."

Jug reached inside his vest and brought out an envelope that had been folded from a sheet of paper and sealed with wax. From the thickness, Dunn guessed that the letter itself was on a second sheet of paper, inside. Even a snoopy person would have a hard time reading a word.

Dunn saddled his horse and set out. He was riding his horse for the fourth day in a row, but he had not worked him hard. The landscape had not changed from the day before, and neither had the weather. The temperature hovered at a little above freezing, just cold enough for Dunn to see his breath if he made the effort.

Percy appeared in the doorway of the bunkhouse as Dunn was tying up his horse. "What brings you here?" he asked.

"A message." Dunn reached into his coat pocket and drew out the envelope. When he reached the front step, he handed it to the boss.

"Thanks. I'll take it in and read it. I imagine he expects an answer, so I'll be out with one in a few minutes."

"I'll wait here."

"Sure."

Percy reappeared in about five minutes. He handed Dunn an envelope formed like the other one but made of paper with a duller shade. "You can tell him I burned his."

"I will." Dunn put the envelope in his coat pocket.

"Good enough." Percy waited at the door until Dunn mounted up and turned away.

Out on the trail, Dunn reviewed the brief visit and shrugged. Not only had Percy let him wait outside, but no one told him anything. He imagined the latter part was for the better. If anyone questioned him, he could say in truth that he knew nothing. But he had an idea of how these things worked, and he imagined that before long, a small crew of riders would show up at the way station, hustling a herd of jiggling cattle.

The grey horse that Verna rode was grazing by itself in the pasture when Dunn put his horse away. He knocked on the door of the cookshack, and Verna called for him to come in. He imagined she had seen him when he rode in. She would not have been so casual with the knock of some wayfarer.

He took off his hat as he went in and closed the door behind him. The room was neither warm nor cold, and the light consisted of what came in through the window. Verna was seated at the table, wearing a dark blue sweater, with her dark hair hanging loose to her shoulders. Her hands were in her lap, and a tan crockery mug sat on the table in front of her. She raised her hand to touch the hair at the side of her head.

"The boys are still out. I thought I would wait till they came back, and I would heat up some dinner."

"I'm in no hurry."

"There's some coffee left. Lukewarm, I think."

"That would be all right."

"I'll pour it. Have a seat."

He pulled the unoccupied bench away from the table and set his hat next to him as he sat down. Verna rose, moved into the dimmer light, and returned with a tin cup like the ones the men had been drinking from. She kept the table between them as she set the cup in front of him.

"Thanks," he said. He stifled a yawn. He felt himself beginning to relax.

"A small thing. I'll make some more when I build up a fire." She gave a shrug, almost a flinch. "I thought they'd be back by now, but you never know."

"That's life on the range. Sometimes the work takes longer." He sipped the coffee. It was almost cold, but it tasted all right.

"They don't tell me much about their work, so I don't know what they went out to do today."

"It shouldn't matter. And I mean that in a positive way. Sometimes it's better not to know."

"You mean details."

"Well, yes. But I have to admit, even in my own case, if I don't know the details, I still have a general idea."

Her hazel eyes met his. "You don't seem as deep into it as these others do."

He shrugged. "I don't know that much about them. I imagine you've noticed that they don't tell me all that much, either."

After a couple of seconds of silence, she said, "You could get out if you wanted."

His eyes roved over her. She was attractive in face and figure, and she still held her youth. He could not tell if she was speaking out of envy, encouragement, or some other sentiment he was yet to recognize. "I think you're right," he said, "but it's not easy. I'm sure you know what I mean when I say that something holds a person in a place like this. Even in my case, where that something is not very strong, it's easier to go along than it is to resist—even when you think, or you think you know, that there's got to be a better way to get along in life."

"That's a good way of putting it. You have to want to leave pretty bad, and even then, I don't know if I—"

The pounding of hoofbeats came to a stop, and a sharp voice carried, though Dunn did not catch the words. He stood up from the bench and took hold of his hat with one hand and the tin cup with the other.

Jug stormed in and stopped short, glaring at Dunn. "Oh, you're here." He turned to Verna, who had also stood up. "What have you been talking about?"

Dunn admired her calm voice as she said, "Work."

"Is that right?"

"Yes. I was telling him how when we were little, they always drummed it into us that all work was good work."

"Hah. If it was good, more people would like it."

Dunn tipped up his cup and drank half of the coffee. "Do you want me to go out and help with the horses?"

"No, you can wait here. The boys can take care of it."

Dunn remembered the envelope. He took it out and handed it to Jug. "Here's this."

"Thanks." Jug stuffed the envelope in his hip pocket.

Verna moved a couple of steps. "I'll start a fire and heat up the rest of the beans."

"Do that." Jug seethed as he turned his head toward the voices outside. "Of all the sonsabitchin'—"

"Did something go wrong?" Verna asked.

"Wrong? If things went right, we wouldn't be in this dump."

Dunn made himself not look at Verna. For the time being, at least, it was just as well that they had not gone any further in their conversation. But it hadn't taken much for her to talk about getting out.

One of the horses was dead when Dunn went out to check on them after the midday dinner. The sorrel with no markings had its mouth open and its eye wide to the sky. To be sure of its condition, Dunn stood close and nudged a leg with the toe of his boot. The leg sagged back into place.

Dunn stared at the body. The death of a working horse was

no small matter, and it seemed even larger in these tight circumstances. Hunter had been riding the sorrel, but however Jug reassigned the mounts, they were going to be short by one.

Jug did not seem surprised when Dunn reported to him. He was seated at the table with the other two men, and Dunn had the impression that he had interrupted a serious conversation.

"Drag it to the far end of the canyon. The three of you. Rod, you can ride the grey horse."

Stanberry and Hunter did not offer any explanations as the three men went about the task. Stanberry put a rope around one hind leg, and Hunter tied onto the other. Dunn tied the front legs together, mounted up, and waited to stay behind to steer. The floor of the canyon was pocked from cattle that had grazed there when the ground was wet, so the dead weight had resistance from the surface. The party had not gone fifty yards when the carcass hung up on a low spot. Dunn pulled his end to one side, and when the others started up again, the dead horse turned over. The front quarter that had been lying on the ground was now uppermost, soaked with blood and matted with dirt. Stanberry and Hunter dragged on.

In the cookshack once again, with the horses put away for the second time, Dunn expected that Jug would say something to wrap up this recent turn of events. A bottle of whiskey appeared, and Dunn took a shot in a tin cup with the others. All four men and Verna were standing, at a yard or two distance from one another, but no one spoke.

After a few seconds, Dunn took the initiative. "Does this mean we're going to have someone down our necks?"

Jug narrowed his eyes. "It doesn't have to mean anything in particular. And you don't need to know anything more than I tell you."

Verna was standing between Jug and the stove with her hands on her hips. "He's got a right to know what's going on."

Jug's arm came up as if by impulse, and he backhanded her. She backed up and put her hand to her mouth where he had hit her.

Dunn boiled up. He did not think he could cross the line and tell a man what to do with his woman, but for the first time, he thought he could lift a hand toward Jug if it came to it.

Jug's chest rose, and he heaved out a long breath. His face was cloudy, but his voice was deliberate. "Everyone needs to stay in their places. No questions, no voluntary ideas. We have work comin' up, and we need to keep order to do it."

III

Jug had an annoyed expression on his face as he opened and closed his hand and stared at it. Most of the time, the men did not talk much during meals, but Stanberry and Hunter had been bickering all through breakfast about a hand of poker at some time in the past. Hunter had run out of chips, so there was a side pot. They were playing a split-pot game, dealer's choice, with the low hand taking half and the high hand taking half. Hunter had tied with another player named Skylar for the low hand, but Skylar had bet all the way through, so there had been a big argument about how to divvy up the two pots among the three players. Hunter insisted he had been beaten out of a large amount of money, and Stanberry, who had held the high hand, argued that everything had come out fair and square.

Jug slapped his hand on the table, and the others flinched. "Aw, why don't the two of you dry up? That happened a long time ago, Skylar's dead and gone, and you would have pissed the money away even if they had given it to you, which it seems to me they shouldn't have, anyway."

"It wasn't the money. It was the principle of the thing."

"Oh, lay off of it. I don't know how many times I've heard this story." Jug turned to Dunn. "You might as well work on firewood this morning. The stack's going down. I'll see what's doin' for the rest of the day."

"Will do." Dunn finished his coffee and stood up. He exchanged a glance with Verna as he picked up the ax from the corner.

Hunter's voice had a sulky tone as he said, "We need to see about gettin' another horse."

Jug said, "We'll talk about it."

Stanberry and Hunter were playing cards when Dunn came in at noon. Stanberry sat on the bench next to Jug, and Hunter sat across from him in his usual place. Jug was sharpening the knife that Verna used to slice bacon.

Stanberry pushed a pile of cards toward Hunter. "That's enough for me. We've just about worn the spots off of those cards."

"You don't like to lose," said Hunter.

"Nobody does."

Dunn set the ax in the corner, hung his hat on a nail, and stood aside. "I've got it all cut. I can bring it in after dinner."

Jug did not look up as he said, "You can go ahead and bring it in now. I've got somethin' else for you to do after dinner." He sniffed. "Art and Rod will help you. Go ahead, boys." He looked up with a calm expression on his face. "See anything?"

"No," said Dunn.

"Well, we've got to keep a lookout, you know."

Dunn finished his fried potatoes and bacon and drank a cup of coffee, waiting for Jug's orders. He had noticed that Jug's methods of authority included changing people's plans, taking up their time, and making them wait. At the moment, Dunn also had an undercurrent of worry that Jug was going to try to appropriate his horse. He had thought of that possibility when

197

he was cutting wood, and he had returned to it when it seemed that Stanberry and Hunter were ignoring him more than usual.

Jug laid his knife down after picking his teeth with it. He had been using his left hand, as he had done when he was sharpening the kitchen knife earlier. He turned to Dunn and said, "I'm going to send you up to McFarland's again. I don't need to send a letter. I think it'll be more effective if you just tell him we need to borrow a horse from him."

"Borrow a horse?"

"That's right. It's just that simple. If he asks why, tell him one of ours died. That's all you know, anyway."

"He might have all of his turned out."

"Tell him we need one. You might have to go out and catch it."

Dunn took a breath. "All right. I will."

Percy was standing outside, bareheaded, when Dunn rode into the yard. "Back again?"

"Yep." Dunn swung down and stepped forward with the dark horse at his elbow. "Jug sent me to tell you that he needs to borrow a horse."

Percy's face went sour. "I can't do that. Tell him all of my horses are out to winter pasture."

"I told him they might be. He said I could go out and catch one."

"I can't. All of my horses have my brand. You know that. And I don't have that many to spare. What's he need one for, anyway?"

"One of theirs died."

Percy looked at the ground and shook his head. "Tell him I'm sorry, but I can't. Of all the things, he ought to be able to find a horse somewhere. You don't need to repeat the last part. Or the part about the brand."

"I won't."

"I appreciate it." After a pause, Percy added, "I don't know why it's takin' so long."

Dunn shrugged. "I have no idea."

"Tomorrow's Sunday. It's been almost a week."

"I don't know."

"Well, I'll let you go. Water your horse if you want."

"I will."

A mile from the ranch, Dunn decided to go back by way of town. He wasn't expected back at any specific time, and, as he reasoned with himself, no one had told him not to go through town. A change of scenery might do him some good, and then he would be back at the outlaw camp as usual, with its tension and bickering.

He figured the time at midafternoon as he rode down the main street of Brigstock. Three horses were tied in front of the Hitching Post Saloon, but the area in front of the café down the street was vacant. Dunn thought he might have timed his visit well again.

Milly was wiping the counter when he walked in with the doorbell tinkling overhead. She raised her head and stood back a step as he walked between the two rows of tables.

"Good afternoon, Joe. What can I do for you? Coffee?"

He slowed. She was treating him like a regular customer. "I just dropped in to see how you're doing."

She held her hands together in front of her. "Well enough, I suppose."

He stopped a few feet from the counter. "Do you ever get away from here?"

She shook her head. "Not to speak of. And yourself? Work going all right?"

"The same. Not much happening."

"Must be the same all over." She folded her arms.

"Heard any news?"

"Not since I saw you last."

"Are you pretty busy right now?"

"You know me. I'm always busy. Getting ready right now for the evening customers."

"I see. Well, I won't take up any more of your time."

"It's no trouble. Come again."

On the street, Dunn felt as if he had walked in the door and out. She hadn't treated him like a Romeo with two bits, but he hadn't gotten close enough to smell her perfume, either. She must not be trying to keep him like a fish on the line.

He glanced at the sky. The light spot in the cloud cover had not moved. He had time for one beer, and he could not know when the next chance might come around.

Three young cowpunchers stood at the bar in the Hitching Post Saloon. They were all cleaned up, dressed in bandanas, bright shirts, and wrist cuffs. They laughed and chattered, and from their comments, Dunn understood that they had just been paid off. Every few minutes, one of them would sing a line or two from a song, and the others would join in and drown out any clear words. Dunn recognized tunes he had heard in the bunkhouses and roundup camps. First it was, "And he said hot biscuits soon be on the way." Next he heard, "Now all you fair maidens where'er you reside," in an artificial high voice like a woman's. Then in a stately tone and sonorous voice came the words, "And I rode him for seasons on the wide grassy plain." No one joined in on this last verse. The singer raised his glass and said, "I never have drank before, but I think I'll have one now." They all laughed, and their talk went on.

Dunn enjoyed the good cheer of the moment. At the same time, he wondered how free of care or guilt anyone was. As he knew life, everyone had trouble and sorrows. Then again, most of the people he knew of late were crooked or low on principles. Even if these young cowpunchers were not carefree all the time, he appreciated the contrast. There were people, even on the range, who did not have to drag a dead horse away from the common eye while they were waiting to pull a job.

The sky was clearing at sunset when Dunn put his horse in the pasture. The other three horses were grazing. They looked up but did not come to the gate as they sometimes did.

Inside the cookshack, the air was warm and close, as Verna was frying salt pork. She exchanged a quick glance with Dunn as he hung up his hat and coat. He moved around and stood at the end of the table so he wouldn't be standing behind anyone.

"Well, let's have it," said Jug.

"Percy said he didn't have a horse to spare."

"What the hell? He's got to have eight or ten."

"He said they were all out."

"You could have went and got one."

"I mentioned it, as you did."

Jug made a spitting sound. "He just didn't want to."

Dunn practiced not saying anything.

"What took you so long, then, if you didn't bring a horse?"

"I stopped in town and drank one beer."

"Oh, you did? You let yourself be seen, and I suppose you were mooning around the café, blabbing."

"There wasn't much conversation to be had there."

"Just as well."

Hunter said, "We're still short one horse."

"Of course we are," Jug snapped. He peeled off a cigarette paper and opened his sack of tobacco.

Jug raised his eyelids and stared at his fingers as he rolled a cigarette. He held his liquor better than the other two did, but an air of dullness hung all around the table. Each of the men had a tin cup in front of him, and a near-empty whiskey bottle sat on the table between them.

Verna was not using the stump at present, so Dunn rolled it away from the heat of the stove and sat on it. He did not enjoy the company of drunk and surly men, but he had been around men like that before, sometimes in the same condition himself, and he was not going to miss a meal because of unpleasant company.

Dunn had just fallen asleep when Stanberry and Hunter came in from the shack next door. Before long, both of them were snoring and blubbering. Dunn turned over one way and the other, but he could not go back to sleep. The sounds of the other two men aggravated him more and more until he had enough. He threw off the covers, then took more care to be quiet as he put on his clothes and found his hat and coat. His boots had spurs on them, so he put on a pair of old worn slippers that he used around camp.

The sky was clear, so the night was cold, but he was glad to be outside. No light showed in the building next door, so he did not feel that he had to walk far to be alone.

The moon, between a quarter and a half, shed enough light for him to gaze across the landscape. He could feel his aggravation going down. All he had to do was stick things out a little longer, make some money on this deal, and decide on his next move. He had been stuck deeper. Nothing lasted that long.

The scuff of a door opening turned him around. Someone was coming out of the cookshack but not very fast. Half a minute later, moonlight showed a dark head of hair and a woman's form wrapped in a sweater.

He waited for her to walk up to him.

"I heard someone go out," she whispered. "I thought it was you."

"Those other two are dead asleep."

"So is Jug. Let's walk a little farther away."

Fifty yards out did not seem like much when there was nothing else around for miles. "Let's go a little ways more," he said.

At about a hundred yards, they stopped.

"I can't stand it," she said.

"That's you and me both. I wish something would happen, and we could get this job done."

"That's just part of it. But at least you could leave."

"You could, too, if you wanted." He felt that they were picking up the conversation where they had left off a day and a half before.

"Of course I want out, but I don't know if I can do it. Like you said before, there's something that holds us here. And of course it's different for me than it is for you."

He didn't want to talk about some of that, but he had other thoughts, so he said, "I'll just speak for myself. Here's how I see it. No one can go on like this forever. But he's got to decide not to. Someone who doesn't decide that he doesn't want to do this—that is, be a criminal—has a dead-end future to look forward to." He took a breath. "On the other hand, someone who just walks out on a gang can expect a bullet in the back. So he's got to pick his time, and for me, that's the end of this job, when I ought to have some money to go on as well."

"It sounds like you've got it thought out. You know what you want."

He turned to her. He wanted to put his hands on her shoulders, but he restrained himself. "I'm not a deep thinker, but sometimes I can sort things out. This may be one of the last chances I get to start over. I don't want to think of it or speak of it as my last chance, because if I think I'm at that point, I might do something rash. But I think I'm next to it."

"Next to the last chance."

"Something like that. But I have to keep my head about me."

She took a breath and seemed to be gathering her words. "If you can get out—" Her voice was shaky, and she started again. "If you can get out, I'd like to try to do the same thing."

"Together?"

"I don't know. I'm sure I couldn't do it first, and I don't know if I can do it on my own. I think that if I tried to walk out when you did, it would be too big of a fight, too much trouble. But if you go first, I might be able to . . ."

"Catch up with me?"

"Maybe, but I don't know how."

"Well, I know what I want to do, so here's an idea. If I get out all right, I'll be at a place called Glover Canyon. It's south of town and almost due east of here, about ten miles."

"That's a long ways to make it on my own."

"I can always see about coming back for you, but that's full of problems."

"That's for sure."

"Well, we'll see what happens." He wanted to take her in his arms, but something told him not to. It wasn't the shiver of thinking that someone could walk up behind him and put a gun to his head; for one thing, he was facing the way station. What spoke to him was the basic lesson of his life, the knowledge that if he didn't look out for himself first, he wouldn't be of any use to anyone, including himself. And looking out for himself, at this moment, meant not giving in.

"What's your last name?" he asked.

"It's Delorme. Not very many people ask."

"It seems like something I should know about someone I'd like to see again."

Her voice had a slight quaver as she said, "I would like that, too." She turned and glanced at the station. "We should be going back."

"You're right." He did not know how tough he really was. He realized he could have given in even after he had decided not to. But the moment was past. Now it was just simple caution. "I'll let you go first, so we don't go in together. When I think it's clear, I'll go."

"That's a good idea. Good night."

"And the same to you. Take care."

Bleak sunlight fell on the rangeland around the way station. Dunn had been sitting on the front step for almost two hours, watching without expecting anything in particular. He heard Jug open the back door of the other shack, clear his throat with great effort, and spit. Within a few minutes, Dunn heard the muttered voices of Stanberry and Hunter. He imagined Verna had been waiting for others to stir, for now came the clanking sound of opening and closing the cast-iron stove and setting cast-iron skillets on the stove top.

The hotcakes were thin, and the molasses ran out. Stanberry asked if someone needed to go for supplies.

Jug said, "Everyone needs to stay around here today. We need to be ready."

Through the rest of the morning and into the afternoon, the men loitered around the buildings, walked here and there, and kept an eye to the north. Dunn did not know if the cattle would come from Percy's place, but he guessed that they would pass by that way at least. He knew better than to ask questions. Whatever was going to happen would do so in its own time.

Breakfast had been so late that dinner came around at about three in the afternoon. The meal consisted of fried potatoes with the memory of pork, carried in the grease.

"This is dinner and supper together," said Jug. "You never know when they'll get here."

Dunn wondered if Jug had received some new communication, and by what means, as Percy had not seemed to know anything specific the day before. Dunn recalled that today was Sunday, and he did not know if it made any difference.

The second half of the afternoon dragged on, and still nothing appeared. Dunn wandered back and forth to check on the horses. He did not work on firewood because the supply was adequate and he did not know how much longer they would stay at this camp. Stanberry and Hunter continued to walk around and to cast glances to the north. They reminded Dunn of men waiting for a steam whistle, but this station was miles away from any town or railroad track.

Darkness fell. The men gathered in the cookshack, even though no meal was forthcoming. Dunn thought Jug was making a show of being calm. The boss was rolling a cigarette, and his eyelids were relaxed as he looked down at his work.

"This is the way it goes sometimes. You just have to be able to wait. You-all can try to get some sleep if you want, but when the time comes, you need to be ready to go."

After a while, Dunn made his way in the dark to the other shack. Still dressed, he stretched out on his bed with one blanket to cover him.

He awoke in the darkness with the single blanket on top of him. The rumble of hooves carried through the floor. He turned the blanket aside and sat up. The drumming sound came through the wall. It did not sound like the lumbering thud of cattle. The animals were moving fast and coming closer.

As he pulled on his boots, he heard voices outside. Jug was telling the others to open the pasture gate. Dunn put on his hat and coat and stepped outside to see a stream of galloping horses pass behind the shack. At the very end, a rider rushed by, hollering, *"Hee-yah! Hee yah!"*

Dunn heard nickering and grunting at the hitching rail

between the two buildings. As the herd of horses thundered into the pasture, Dunn picked his way behind the shack in the moonlight and came around the corner to face his horse and Verna's tied at the rail. He did not make sense of it to begin with, and his reasoning was cluttered with resentment that someone had handled his horse without asking him. His earlier suspicion rose. They were going to try to take his horse.

Everything was up in the air at the moment—horses milling and neighing and whinnying in the pasture, men's voices, and now two riders loping back in the direction they had come from. Dunn was trying to think of what he should be ready for when Jug's voice sounded behind him.

"Hurry up and get your horse ready. You're goin' with this bunch."

Half of it made sense. They had taken his horse from the pasture in order to have it out of the way and ready.

"Who else is going?" he asked.

"Rod."

"Just two?"

"That's all it takes. We need two to stay here."

Dunn's mind cleared as he hurried inside for his gear. He would be traveling fast, so he needed to go light. He would use two saddle blankets as always, but he would leave the rifle and scabbard. His gloves were in his coat pocket. Ah, yes. His pistol and holster.

He buckled on his gunbelt, saw that his canteen was in the saddlebag, and grabbed his saddle and blankets. The bridle was draped on the saddle horn, and his rope was tied to the offside where it should be. That was good. The stirrups flopped as he hurried to the door and stepped outside.

The dark horse stood still as Dunn laid the blankets on with one hand, smoothed them, swung the saddle up, and settled it into place. He worked fast, but he took care to make sure every detail was right. He couldn't have anything slipping or loosening on this job.

He heard movement behind him, then Hunter's voice as the man talked to the grey horse and saddled it.

Dunn worked the bridle onto his horse's head, settled the bit between the teeth, and untied the lead rope from the horse's neck. He left the rope looped on the hitching rail and led the horse out. He took it a little farther than the usual six or eight steps, just to be sure, and tightened the cinch a notch.

Jug reappeared in the darkness as Hunter was catching up with the grey horse in tow. As usual, Jug was curt with his orders.

"Rod's gonna ride in the lead. He knows the way. You move fast. That's always the way with horses. Dunn, you take up the drag. Don't let anything wander from the bunch, although they usually don't if you keep 'em goin' fast."

"I've moved horses before."

"Good. Just take 'em to the next place, leave 'em off, and come back. Now get ready. I'll tell Art, and he'll open the gate. He's got our other two horses tied up." Jug was about to turn, and he stopped. "What do you want?"

Verna's shape was visible in the moonlight. "A little food for them to take along. Just some cold biscuits."

"Make it quick." Jug lingered, took a couple of steps, and stopped. He turned and watched.

Verna came forward, handed an object to Hunter, and walked around the rear of the grey horse to approach Dunn. She held forward a small bundle. It looked as if it had a couple of biscuits wrapped in a cloth torn from a bedsheet.

Dunn was about to say thanks when she dropped the bundle.

"Oh! I'm sorry." She knelt to pick up the items. As he bent to receive them, she whispered, "Be careful who you ride with."

"Thanks," he said as he stood up.

"You're welcome." She turned and walked away.

He put the cloth and biscuits in his coat pocket and took a deep breath. He turned out his stirrup, put the toe of his boot in place, grabbed the saddle horn, and swung aboard. When his right foot found the stirrup, he saw that Hunter was already loping out ahead.

Stanberry had the gate open, and the horses began to pour through. Dunn could not see color, but he could see that the herd had a usual mix of bays, buckskins, browns, sorrels, darks, greys, whites, and a couple of palominos. He could not see brands, and he had no idea of whether these horses all came from the same outfit. He estimated about fifty head, and he knew that big outfits often had more than a hundred. This was a large group for two men herding in the dark, but two riders had brought them, and Hunter knew the way.

From time to time, as the trail turned, Dunn could see Hunter in the lead, loping at a steady pace on the grey horse. Dunn had to slow down and speed up as horses fell back or drifted to one side. At least the ground did not give them much trouble, as the trail led through an even rangeland of sagebrush and grass, with hills and low buttes showing from time to time on the right.

The ride seemed to go on forever. Dunn did not like to lope his horse for so long without a rest, even though he changed leads. But if he slowed to give his horse a breather, he would have to race to catch up.

He wondered how many relays there were in total, and how many riders. Fifty horses could bring in a fair amount of money, but when it was split up among a dozen men or more, an individual like himself was not going to end up with much. Maybe there would be another relay, or more.

The horses began to slow and curve to the right, toward a low bluff. A man on horseback came into view on the right, then a man on his left holding two strands of rope, ready to close off a rope corral. Dunn sagged back and let the horses run ahead. He turned around and trotted back, and the man with the ropes gave him a space to pass by.

He let his horse walk to catch its breath. He rode in a circle so that Hunter could catch up and find him. He hoped Hunter did not want to travel too fast on the way back. The night was still dark. He had to have his wits about him, for he was on his own with Hunter now.

The dark horse's neck was wet with sweat. Dunn had to keep the animal moving so it would not cool down too fast and take sick that way. The more Dunn thought about it, the more he was convinced that he did not want to make another run like this one.

The grey horse materialized out of the darkness. Hunter fell in beside Dunn, and the two of them headed north.

Hunter said, "Well, we got that little job done."

"Good thing. I hope it wasn't too hard on these horses."

"Oh, they'll be all right."

The two rode on. Hunter was riding on Dunn's left side, and he kept reining his horse to keep it half a length behind. The grey horse was the type that liked to stay even, so it picked up its pace each time to catch up.

Dunn thought about stopping and telling Hunter that he wanted him to ride even. He decided to stop once and say nothing to give him the idea.

They moved on again, and Hunter continued to fall back. Dunn decided he would stop, turn his horse, back up to the side, and tell Hunter. As he did, Hunter stopped the grey horse and spoke.

"This is far enough, chum."

Dunn was ready. As he drew his pistol, he saw motion and heard a click. He eared back the hammer and aimed at the dark form on the back of the light horse. He saw the flame and heard the blast of Hunter's six-gun as he himself pulled the trigger. The air cracked and *whoofed* near his left cheek, and he heard the *whop* of his shot go home.

The grey horse squealed and bolted, dumping Hunter in the dirt. Dunn held fast on the reins of the dark horse and brought the animal under control. He waited to see if Hunter moved, but the body lay still. Searching around, Dunn saw a spot of light color less than a hundred yards away.

By the time he laid hands on the reins of the grey horse, Dunn had decided not to load the body. He did not want to struggle with the dead weight and try to manage two horses out in the middle of nowhere with nothing to tie them to. He had a bird in the hand, as the saying went, and he did not want to still be out here when daylight came. He nodded to himself. Leading the grey horse, he set out for the way station.

IV

The small, weathered buildings came into view as dull light began to spill over the plain. A thin haze hung in the sky as before, and the air was still. The wind often picked up at midmorning at this time of year, so Dunn saw the stillness as something temporary. He also knew that as soon as he rode into the robbers' roost with an empty horse at his side, things would liven up like fire in a skillet of grease.

The phrase "robbers' roost" occurred to him in the first quiet instant that he saw the place that morning, after more than two hours of thinking about the probable treachery of Jug and his cohorts. He was not one of them. They were not his people. Verna might be, and he remembered well her warning. But he needed to think for himself first—to get out clear, with his rifle and other belongings. In order to do that, he knew he could not give an indication that he knew anything. He could not show how much he despised these men and the code of the criminal, the legendary honor among thieves.

Jug came out of the shack, bootheels thumping on the step, as Dunn tied his horse to the rail.

"Where's Rod? What happened?"

Dunn moved to tie the grey horse. With his back to Jug, he said, "Somebody got him."

Jug barked, "Somebody got him? What do you mean?"

Dunn turned and observed the outlaw boss, with his blazing eyes and bloodshot cheeks. "Just that. Someone shot him in the dark. We had left off the herd and were on the way back, walking our horses, taking it slow to let them catch their breath. We had come less than a mile, and out of nowhere there came a shot."

"Rifle or pistol?"

"I tried to think about that later, but I couldn't tell you. It happened all at once, and in the dark, and it was just the one shot. Knocked him clean out of the saddle, though."

"Son of a bitch." Jug bore down on Dunn with his brown eyes. "You didn't have any words with him, did you?"

"Oh, no. We never got to any point like that. We were just poking along. My horse kept getting a little ahead, and when I stopped one time, it happened."

Jug's eyes were bleary as he relaxed them and shook his head. "Son of a bitch. I wonder why they'd shoot *him.*"

"Maybe he made an easier target, riding a light-colored horse."

"And you didn't see anybody? Hear anybody?"

Dunn moved his head in the negative. "No one else. No one at all."

Jug heaved a breath as he looked around and focused on Stanberry, who had stepped out of the other shack. "Rod's been killed. Something went wrong."

Stanberry flinched. "That's no good."

"You damn right it isn't." Jug came back to Dunn. "Why did you just leave him?"

"I didn't know if I could load him, with two horses to hang onto and nothing to tie to, and I didn't want to lose one of them. I had a hard enough time getting a hand on the grey horse. Once I did that, I didn't know who else was out there, or where."

"This is a hell of a mess. If you'd at least have brought him back—"

Dunn did not answer.

"I'll say it's a hell of a mess," said Stanberry. "I want to know who's out to get us. This is supposed to be an even deal."

Jug said, "We don't know. We don't know anything. Just what he tells us." Specks of saliva flew as he said, "Are you sure that's the way it happened?"

"Of course I am."

Verna had come out of the cookshack, fully dressed with her arms crossed and her sweater wrapped close. "You sound like you don't believe him."

Quick as a cat, Jug whipped around and slapped her. "You stay out of this. Go back inside."

Dunn flared up. "Don't you lay another hand on her," he said.

Jug squared his shoulders and rested his fingertips on his belt above his gun and holster. "Don't try to be a buster with me. I'm the wrong one for it. I'll put a bullet through you."

Dunn wanted to say, "Like Hunter tried," but he held his tongue.

Jug turned his head without taking his eye off of Dunn. "I told you to get inside."

Verna walked up the step but did not close the door.

Jug faced Dunn again. "You can pack your gear and leave. Now."

213

"I have pay coming. That was no easy job."

Jug made his spitting sound. "You never worked for us to begin with. Get it from your boss." He made a slow turn and walked away. He clomped the heel of his boot on the step as he went up into the cookshack.

Dunn crossed over to the other building, took a weary step up, and left the door open for light as he went in. He packed his duffel bag first. When he took it outside to set it on the ground, he saw that the grey horse was gone, as was Stanberry. He went inside again and rolled up his bed, then carried it out to set it with his bag. He had to stop and make himself think straight. He was tired, and he had to focus on little things such as the sequence in which he would tie his gear onto his saddle.

He made a final trip inside for his rifle and scabbard. He had decided he would strap it on first, so he began there. While he was making the adjustments, Stanberry returned and went into their shack. He came out a minute later and crossed over to the larger building.

Dunn was laying out the saddle strings to tie on his bedroll when Stanberry and Jug stepped down from the cookshack.

Jug spoke. "Art says he has something missing."

"His teeth?" Dunn turned to face the other two.

"Don't get smart. You're not out of here yet. Tell him, Art."

Stanberry cleared his throat and did not look straight at Dunn. "It's my knife. The fancy one that he had his eye on."

Dunn waved his hand. "Oh, go on. I had no interest in that thing. It seemed to delight you, though."

Stanberry narrowed his eyes as he peered at Dunn. "I tell you, it's missing. There's only so many people here, and no one else has a reason to take it."

"Neither do I, and I have a clear conscience about it. But if it's really missing, maybe Hunter took it."

Stanberry's face went stiff. "That's not funny."

"It wasn't meant to be."

Stanberry's chin moved, and it appeared as if he was working his jaws in anger. "I have a hunch we ought to search your bag."

Everything stopped for a moment. Dunn wondered if the stiletto was planted in his bag, but he hadn't seen it when he was packing up, and he didn't think anyone had the chance to stow something when he had the bag outside. And he did not think someone had done something earlier, because he did not think they expected him to return. He was also certain that the knife was not in his bedroll.

Verna had come outside again and was standing by. He knew he might not ever see her again, but he had his pride, and he was going to stick to it.

"Go ahead," he said. "Search my bag and my bedroll, too. Unless someone did a good job of hiding it, I'm sure it's not there." He took a casual glance at Stanberry, whose face was not as flushed as usual. "I don't care to go through someone else's personal belongings, but if you feel you have to, go ahead."

"Search the bag and bedroll both," said Jug. "You never know when someone's bluffin'."

Stanberry picked up the bedroll first. Leaning over, he bent it across his knee every few inches. "It's not in here. It's damn near a foot long." He straightened up and took a breath.

"Hurry up," said Jug. "We've got things to do."

Though no one had said anything more specific, Dunn had a sense that the others would be pulling out as soon as he was gone. They might have been planning to do so all along, but Hunter's death had caused an upheaval.

Stanberry knelt by the bag, settling with effort in his stovepipe boots. He pulled the canvas straps through the slide buckles and opened the bag. He began by sorting through the socks, gloves, and other effects that lay on top of the larger clothing. Then he ran his hand deeper inside, felt along the length of the bag, and pulled his hand out. He pushed himself to his feet and took in a couple of deep breaths. His usual reddish color returned to his face. "I didn't find it," he said.

"Are you sure?" said Jug.

"I'm sure I didn't find it."

"That's what I meant. Any fool can see that you didn't. Let's get goin'. We're just wastin' time."

Dunn caught a glance from Verna as the small gathering began to break up. He wished he hadn't had to allow the other two men the authority to go through his belongings, but he felt as if he had saved face. And now he would be clear of them.

Dunn's eyelids were heavy from having been up all night, and his legs were tired and sore from the long, hard drive, but he made himself hang on as he rode to Percy McFarland's place. He needed to get there before anyone else did, and he had money coming. A man was supposed to be paid after a job.

Percy stepped out of the bunkhouse into the pale sunlight and closed the door behind him. He was wearing a hat and a denim jacket, and he had a pair of work gloves in his hand. His eyes went over the horse and gear and came back to Dunn.

"What are you doing here? You look like hell."

"I feel like it." Dunn heaved his leg up and over, slid to the ground, and caught his balance. He came around in front of the horse, holding the reins.

Percy kept his eyes on him. "What happened?"

"Jug sent me and another fella named Hunter to deliver a herd of horses, about fifty. When we were on our way back, Hunter caught a bullet in the dark. When I got back to the camp, Jug didn't like any of it, so he told me to leave."

"And so you came here."

"Well, for one thing, I should get paid for that job. And unless something has changed, I'm supposed to be working for you all along."

Percy seemed calm for having heard the news. "One thing at a time. I have to wait until they get paid and then pay me. And from what you say, I don't know if someone has queered the deal. You can't trust anyone, you know."

"I should say not. I'll tell you, I'm dead tired from all of this, and I don't care for the way those fellows did things. I'll leave it at that. But I need to get some rest before I can do anything else."

Percy took a few seconds to respond. "I don't know if it's a good idea for you to be around here."

Dunn frowned. "What do you mean?"

"I don't know what happened, and I don't know who's going to be trailing who. I don't want any of this to come back to me."

Dunn stared at the ground. He realized he had just been pretending to work for a living. It was all crooked, everything he had been doing, and he was done with it. He looked up and said, "I'd like to have what I've got coming, then."

Percy scanned the horse again, as if he could learn more from what he saw. "I'll go figure it," he said.

Dunn calculated that he had thirty-seven dollars coming in wages before this last job. When Percy came outside, he held his hand forward with his fingers pointing downward over a small stack of coins. He laid three ten-dollar gold pieces and one five-dollar piece in Dunn's palm.

Dunn did not have to count the coins more than once as he observed them. "I thought it might be a little more."

"That's what it came to."

Dunn paused. He could see he wasn't going to get any more. "Well, thanks for this much."

"You're welcome. And good luck."

As Dunn plodded away on the dark horse, he thought of what they said of a skinflint, that he would sell his own mother. Not Percy. He would shortchange her for two dollars.

Dunn blinked his eyes. He needed to make it to town and find a place to sleep. He could worry about everything else later.

As he rode on, though, he couldn't put everything out of his mind. He thought Percy knew more than he let on. Of course he did in some ways, but he might know more even about this latest mess. It was hard to tell. And then there was the gang at the way station. They might well have pulled out by now, with one man less. Dunn's eyes opened. At least they weren't short one horse any more.

The sun had not yet climbed to the high spot when Dunn rode into the main street of Brigstock with a cold breeze at his back. He needed a place to sleep where nobody would bother him, so he took a room at the Mallory Hotel. When he had his gear in the room, he took his horse to the livery stable. By the time he made it to the room again, he had just enough energy to pull off his boots.

He awoke in the dark. He was still wearing his clothes. He had to think for a moment to remember where he was. Everything was so quiet that it had to be the middle of the night. He sat up on the side of the bed, collecting his thoughts. After a couple of minutes, he rose and took soft steps to the window. The moon was waning; it was close to a quarter now. The town lay in darkness. Even the saloon was shut down.

Most of the world was asleep, or so it seemed. But even in small towns, as well as in remote places across the countryside, not to mention in the cities, this was the time when men sat up drinking and brooding, schemed against the property of others, and took women against their will. Dunn shook his head. He was one step away from getting out of here. Maybe two.

Enough light came in through the window for him to find the pitcher and pour himself a glass of water. He drank it down. The last thing he had eaten was the pair of cold biscuits, in the dark, when he was leading the grey horse. He was not hungry now, but he knew he would be after he slept some more.

Full daylight was showing when he woke again. He made his way to the hotel restaurant, where he ordered a stack of hotcakes with pork sausage on the side. He drank three cups of coffee as he ate his meal.

Still in no hurry, he had a bath and shaved himself. He checked out of his room, paid for his horse's keep, and loaded his gear. For his next step, he tied the horse in front of the general store and went in to buy enough provisions for a couple of days.

He recalled Jug's complaint about allowing himself to be seen, but no one seemed to pay him any special attention. After tying his packages onto his saddle, he walked his horse down the street in the light of midmorning. He tied up at the Hillrose Café and went in.

Two men in town clothes were eating apple pie and chatting in a light tone. They did not look at Dunn as he took a seat on the other side of the café. Milly frowned as she walked his way with a cup and the coffeepot.

"Anything more?" she asked without meeting his eye.

"I'll wait."

She returned to the back of the establishment and busied herself with wiping the counter and straightening the cups and glasses.

The two men paid their bill and left, still without lending any attention to Dunn.

Milly walked down the aisle in rigid steps and stopped to

pour him more coffee. In a low, tense voice, she said, "What are you doing here?"

He looked up and met her gaze. She had a troubled expression on her face, but he did not sense much concern for him. "Not much," he said. "I'm out of work, on my own. I had some time on my hands, so I thought I'd drop in and see if there was any news."

She sounded as if she was speaking through clenched teeth. "I heard someone got killed in a horse-rustling scheme."

He studied her face. "How did you hear that?"

She held her eyes on him, but they showed nothing. "Talk. Bad news travels fast. Like wildfire, as they say." She glanced at the street where his horse stood. "Are you leaving?"

"I ought to be. I'd like to tell you I had a sack full of money, but I can't even get paid for some of the work I did."

"Times are rough."

"Who was it that got killed? Did you hear a name?"

She shook her head. "You know how it is. You never hear more than part of a story."

The doorbell jingled, and a large man walked in. He had dark bags under his eyes, a large girth, and a suit coat like a tent.

Milly turned and put on a smile. "Hello, Si. We missed you earlier."

"I got tied up."

"Order same as always?"

The man nodded and looked around. He let out a weary breath and said, "I'll sit over here."

"Anywhere you want." Milly swung her hips as she picked up her pace on the way to the counter. She laid her hand on a coffee cup and sang out to the kitchen, "One for Si."

Dunn found a good spot in Glover Canyon, out of the wind,

where the sun at midday warmed the sandstone wall. He could expect the night to be cold, but otherwise it was a suitable place for a camp, with firewood, water, and grass. He stripped his horse and set it on a picket to graze.

Before long, he had his camp in order. He sat on his bedroll and leaned back against his saddle, which he had placed on a log. Now that he was sitting still, he could feel the low temperature around him. And this was the warm part of the day. He buttoned his coat.

He was confident that he could stick it out here for a couple of days. He had no one to bother him. As he reviewed his situation, he felt removed from everyone—Milly, Percy, what was left of the gang, and Verna. He felt best about being away from the outlaws and worst about not knowing where Verna was. He had told her he would be here, but he did not think she would show up on her own. It seemed like a good idea at the time. Glover Canyon was the one place where he would want to hole up, but now that he was here, he had his doubts about her. He would like to see her appear, but hoping didn't make things happen.

As he rolled a cigarette, he ran through his sequence of thoughts again. He felt that he was done with all this low business. It was a good feeling. He could just ride away if he wanted to. But he needed to see if the girl had it in her to leave. Some girls didn't. He had seen it before. A bad deal with a man was like glue.

He lit the cigarette and watched the smoke drift away. This was a good place to wait, at least for a while. He had shared some pleasant moments here with Milly, but he was convinced that the time with her was in the past. Now he was waiting for someone who, in all probability, would not show up. But he was away from everyone else, and that was good. He might even get a deer. When he was here in the summer, he had seen a young buck with a sprig of antlers in velvet. The young ones were easier to hunt.

When he finished the cigarette, he pushed himself to his feet. He decided he would walk back into the canyon and keep warm by moving around. While he was at it, he could be on the lookout for deer.

With the rifle in the crook of his arm, he ambled along. When he warmed up, he moved to the shadows. As time passed, however, the air grew cooler, and he walked in the sunshine.

The dark horse was still grazing when he returned to his camp. He slipped his rifle into the scabbard and went about building a fire. The blaze cheered the atmosphere as dusk approached. He put on more sticks, planning to make a bed of coals, cook his grub, and then build the fire back up for warmth.

Shadows were stretching all the way across the canyon when he dug out his skillet, a medium-sized, cast-iron pan that he had not used in a while. He set it on the coals and began to slice bacon. Some people complained about eating the same food all the time, but bacon was good for camp. It kept well, didn't spoil. He had to think about what he would keep the grease in. If he killed a deer, there was nothing better than bacon grease for frying the meat.

The bacon sizzled and sputtered, and the grease melted. Dunn poked the slices and flipped them.

The horse nickered. Dunn looked over his left shoulder as he crouched, and he saw the dark horse in the fading daylight. A crunching sound caused him to look to his right, and there he saw a pair of stovepipe boots.

He tipped his head and recognized the leering face of Art Stanberry, framed by a dark hat silhouetted against the evening sky. Lowering his eyes, he came to the open barrel of Stanberry's six-gun.

"Cookin' enough for two?"

"Might as well. You never know when company might come calling."

"Maybe you was hopin' someone else would show up."

Dunn's mind raced. Only two people would know to look for him here. Milly and Verna. Dunn could not imagine how Jug would have known to squeeze it out of Verna.

"You know what they say about hope. Did you ever find your stiletto?"

"What?"

"Did you ever find your knife? The one with the naked lady. I have something I want to show you."

As he spoke, Dunn rose from his crouch with the skillet in his left hand. When he thought he had the angle right, he flung the hot grease at Stanberry's face. He did not catch him as well as he wanted, though, for Stanberry turned his head and took the burning liquid on the side of his face. He yowled and squinted and threw up his elbow, giving Dunn just enough time to take the skillet in his right hand. As Stanberry rubbed his eye and began to come around with the .45, Dunn swung the skillet and whacked him on the back of the head.

Stanberry dropped like a stone. Dunn stood over him, and when he was sure the man was not going to move again, he went in search of the light-built bay. He found it tied to a leafless chokecherry bush outside the canyon.

This time, he took the effort to load a body onto a horse. The dead weight was clumsy, and the bay horse was skittish, but Dunn snubbed the horse close and tied up a foot, then heaved with brute force until he had the body draped over the saddle. In the process, the red-handled stiletto fell out of a stovepipe boot.

By the time Dunn had the load tied on and his own horse saddled, night had fallen. He took the body to Pickerall Station, which was vacant as he expected. He left the man's hat, gun, and knife all in place with the body in the smaller shack, then put the saddle there as well. After he turned the horse into the pasture, he left the bridle on the saddle horn.

He looked around and listened to the night before he mounted up. The long sleep had done him some good, but he was tired again, and he had to ride back to Glover Canyon in the dark.

V

Little grey birds were flitting to and fro among the bare branches, and grey morning light was softening the shadows around the camp, when Dunn rolled out of bed and put on his hat, coat, and boots. He had slept a few hours with his clothes on. He had gone to sleep with the assumption that he was going to have to pack up his belongings, and the time had come. He would have a fire long enough to boil coffee in a can and to redo the meal he had had to forgo the evening before.

Pale daylight began to show as he brought the dark horse in to be saddled and loaded. Only yesterday he had unpacked with leisure, and now he was looking over his shoulder again. Someone would come looking for him, and he had to stay at least one jump ahead. And he knew he had better keep a good eye on his backtrail as well.

He rode out of Glover Canyon before the sun cleared the eastern wall. The horse snuffled, then moved ahead in the quiet morning. The sound of footfalls did not carry far, but Dunn was conscious of it, along with the horse's breathing.

Out on the plains, he struck a path to the north and a little west. He did not see a need to pass by the way station again, though he hoped that anyone looking for him would detour there and ponder the findings.

After an hour of riding, he came into more familiar terrain. Percy McFarland's place lay to the north, and Dunn drifted among the points on the landscape where he had kept out of sight on his earlier excursions. He took his time, moving and stopping.

His path took him a ways east again, away from a direct route to McFarland's. He had a hunch that Percy was in on this in ways that had not yet become clear, and his hunch included the possibility that Percy was in touch with Jug and would make some move today.

Dunn was peering over a saddle of sandstone, upslope a few feet from his horse, when he had to hold his breath. Less than a half-mile away, two men rode side by side toward town. Dunn recognized Jug on the stocky brown horse and Percy on the sorrel with two white socks.

Dunn breathed. The nature of his hunch had been correct, but he had to reconstruct the probable details. Stanberry had known to look for him at Glover Canyon, and Dunn could not imagine Verna having provided that lead. But Milly could have given the place name to Percy, who conveyed it to Jug and Stanberry. As Dunn pictured it, the knowledge went from town to the ranch, and now Jug and Percy were going from the ranch to town to find out where Stanberry was. Dunn's heartbeat picked up. That meant Verna might be cached at Percy's place.

Dunn's hand had a slight tremble as he led the dark horse down the slope to level ground. He told himself he couldn't assume what he had just conjectured. But it made sense, even unto the possibility that Percy had moved in on Milly. Percy would not have enough motive or nerve to act against Dunn on his own, but Jug could bully him into complying, just as Jug could invite himself and his companions to stay at Percy's headquarters.

Dunn took a deep breath to calm himself. If Verna was at the ranch, she might not want to leave. If that was the case, he could ride away and be done with all of this. If she did want to leave, the trouble might begin all over again.

The grey horse stood in the corral, and Verna came out of the bunkhouse wearing her dark blue sweater as Dunn rode up to the hitching rail. The cold breeze moved loose strands of her hair, and her face carried a worried expression. She raised her hand to hold her hair in place as she spoke.

"You're taking a big risk coming here. They went out to look for Art, but they could be back at any time."

Dunn swung down and held his horse behind him. "Who told them where to find me?"

She frowned. "I don't know. Why?"

"He came looking for me. He didn't have any luck."

"Oh. I didn't know that was where he went."

"Well, someone told him where to look, but I don't want to dwell on that now. I came to get you out of here."

Her face fell. "I don't know if I can."

"You can if you want."

Fear showed on her face, and her voice quavered. "Jug will kill you for this. You've got to get away while you can."

"I came for you, if you want to go."

"I don't know."

He tried to hold her with his eyes. He had rehearsed some of what he had to say, and he gave it a try. "Look. This is a moment we can't go back on. I've decided what I'm going to do, and that's to get out of this life full of chiselers and thieves and double-crossers. I came to see if you want to go with me."

Her lower lip trembled, and she did not speak.

"You said you would. Or that you would like to try."

"I know I did, but I'm no good."

"You didn't tell them where I was, did you?"

"No, but I've gone along with these crooks, and it's as if I'm one myself."

"You don't have to be."

"And I'm no angel."

He knew what she meant, being Jug's woman. He did not want to dwell on that, either. He found her eyes and said, "I've pulled some crooked things myself, and I can't change what I've been. But I can change what I do from now on. The way I see it, we're two people with flaws, but they don't have to ruin everything. We just don't lie to ourselves or to each other."

Her voice was still unsteady, but her words held together. "Jug will kill you if he can, and he would beat me within an inch of my life, just for talking to you."

"We can't let him."

"Let me decide." She turned and went inside.

Dunn fidgeted and kept an eye all around. Jug would not scruple to shoot him in the back.

Minutes dragged on. Each time Dunn looked around, he expected to see Jug and Percy coming in at a gallop.

The bunkhouse door opened, and Verna took a long step out, swinging the brown leather valise she had carried the first night Dunn saw her.

Dunn's pulse jumped. She had the nerve. "I'll go get the horse," he said.

He hurried through the process of catching the grey horse, brushing it, and putting on the saddle and bridle. As he led the animal across the yard, movement caught his eye, and his heart thumped in his stomach.

Jug was riding in at a dead run by himself, raising dust that carried away in the wind. The horse hooves drummed, slowed, and stopped as Jug piled off. His drover coat settled around him as he stepped forward and spoke in a commanding voice.

"And where do you think you're going, Miss Puss?"

Dunn continued leading the horse with his left hand. With

his right elbow he pushed his coat back, and his hand hovered near the grip of his pistol.

Jug had his left hand in his coat pocket. He raised his chin and turned to regard Dunn. "Put the horse away, sonny boy. No one's going anywhere."

"I am," said Verna.

His eyes shifted to her. "You think you are. But you're wrong."

The brown horse had moved away with its reins trailing on the ground. Jug stood like an actor on stage, with his right hand held out.

"Don't think you can be stubborn with me," he said. "Take your bag inside."

Verna put her hands together. Dunn could see that she was shaking, and he thought she was capable of going back, even now.

Jug began to open and close his right hand, but Dunn kept his eye on the left, which came out of the coat pocket with a nickel-plated pistol.

Dunn drew and fired, but his aim was not perfect. The bullet hit Jug in the face instead of the chest.

Jug fell over backward with his arms out, and the shiny gun tumbled to the ground.

Dunn walked forward and stood for a long moment next to Verna, letting his heartbeat go down.

"He would have killed you," she said.

"I know. He sure tried."

She nodded and did not look down at the body.

Dunn wanted to say that it was over now, but he took the opportunity to say less. "I think we should move him inside."

All the way to town, Dunn had an uncertain sense about Verna. He thought she was capable of going back, even though there was nothing to go back to except the dead hand of bondage. He imagined she still had some feeling for Jug as well, and he did not want to intrude upon what he imagined was her grief. So he let her ride in silence.

At the edge of town, he said, "I need to find Percy if I can. Before I do, I have a couple of questions."

She moistened her lips. "Go ahead."

"What was his last name?"

"Martin. Jug Martin. I think Jugwald was an old family name." She seemed to be reviewing her thoughts, but she said, as before, "He would have killed you."

"I knew he would try. But I remembered what he did with his hands. I had seen him use his left hand, and I figured his right hand cramping up was all a show."

"I think it was. He was proud that he could do things with either hand, like throw a baseball or pitch horseshoes."

"Vain."

"That was a word for him. He was vain about his face. It was better looking when he was younger, before I met him, but he still didn't like anyone scratching it or hitting it in a fight." As the horses walked on, she said, "Did you have another question?"

"It's of a different nature."

She nodded.

"Right there at the end—was your mind made up?"

Her voice was steady as she said, "Yes, it was. He might have been able to break me one more time, but I didn't want him to." After a pause, she said, "Nothing is easy."

"I'll agree with you on that. Let's go this way."

They turned onto the main street, and Dunn saw the sorrel horse with two white socks tied up in front of the café. He led the way and drew rein as Percy McFarland stepped outside and put on his hat. The sound of the doorbell died as he closed the door behind him.

Dunn swung down from his horse. He did not expect trouble with Percy, but he wanted to stand clear. Percy stayed on the sidewalk, in the shade of the awning, with his hands at his sides. Milly appeared behind him on the other side of the glass.

Percy's head moved back and forth, and his voice came out. "What's on your mind, Joe?"

"Not much."

"You might be traveling in dangerous company."

"Thanks for looking out for me. I just dropped by to let you know that you might want to go out and pick up things at your place."

Percy's eyes went to the woman and the grey horse again. "I see. Thanks for the word."

"Don't mention it." Dunn led his horse into the middle of the street under a bright sky. He set his foot in the stirrup, pulled himself up, and swung his leg high and over. As he settled in and caught the other stirrup, his eyes met Verna's.

"Ready?" he asked.

"Yes, I am."

She fell in beside him, and they moved out at a brisk walk. The grey horse kept pace with the dark one as the man and the woman rode away.

ABOUT THE AUTHOR

John D. Nesbitt is the author of more than forty books, including traditional westerns, crossover western mysteries, contemporary western fiction, retro/noir fiction, nonfiction, and poetry. He has won the Western Writers of America Spur Award four times—twice for paperback novel, once for short story, and once for poem. He has won the Western Fictioneers Peacemaker Award twice—once for novel and once for short story. He has been a finalist for the Spur Award twice, the Peacemaker four times, and the Will Rogers Medallion Award six times. He has also received two creative writing fellowships with the Wyoming Arts Council—once for fiction, once for nonfiction. Recent works include *Great Lonesome* and *Silver Grass,* both with Five Star. Visit his website at www.johndnesbitt.com

The employees of Five Star Publishing hope you have enjoyed this book.

Our Five Star novels explore little-known chapters from America's history, stories told from unique perspectives that will entertain a broad range of readers.

Other Five Star books are available at your local library, bookstore, all major book distributors, and directly from Five Star/Gale.

Connect with Five Star Publishing

Website:
   gale.com/five-star

Facebook:
   facebook.com/FiveStarCengage

Twitter:
   twitter.com/FiveStarCengage

Email:
   FiveStar@cengage.com

For information about titles and placing orders:
   (800) 223-1244
   gale.orders@cengage.com

To share your comments, write to us:
   Five Star Publishing
   Attn: Publisher
   10 Water St., Suite 310
   Waterville, ME 04901